Taste For
TEMPTATION

PHYLLIS BOURNE

HARLEQUIN®
entertain, enrich, inspire™

For author Farrah Rochon,
for her support, encouragement and friendship.

And as always, for Byron, who makes
my real life happily-ever-after sweeter than any romance novel.

Recycling programs
for this product may
not exist in your area.

ISBN-13: 978-0-373-86283-2

TASTE FOR TEMPTATION

Copyright © 2012 by Phyllis Bourne Williams

www.Harlequin.com

Printed in U.S.A.

Dear Reader,

As an author, I'm often asked if any of my books contain a slice from my real life. The answer has always been no—up until now.

While writing *Taste for Temptation,* I did a stint in workout boot camp alongside my dieting heroine, Brandi Collins. So I guarantee the aches and pains that accompanied every leg squat, sit-up and excruciating push-up are absolutely authentic.

Fortunately, my research wasn't all killer workouts.

Brandi's neighbor, Adam Ellison, gave me an opportunity to develop my nonexistent baking skills in classes where I learned to make a variety of chocolate-based desserts, including lava cake and éclairs. The heavenly smells coming from the classroom's oven made it easy to understand how Brandi could find her willpower waning in the face of a gorgeous man bearing melt-in-your-mouth yumminess.

I hope you enjoy Brandi and Adam's story. Look for the second Ellison brother Kyle's story next year.

Best wishes,

Phyllis

Chapter 1

"Come on, just one more. You can do it!"

Brandi Collins hoisted her upper body on quivering arms. She held the position less than a second before collapsing face-first in the grass.

"Good job on push-ups, ladies," the trainer shouted at the ten women in the boot camp workout class. "Now flip over and give me two sets of crunches."

Brandi spit blades of dead grass from her mouth and rolled gingerly onto her back. She stared through bare-limbed trees at the gray sky, the hard ground a welcome reprieve from endless push-ups, wind sprints and jumping jacks.

"Let's go, Brandi! This is boot camp, not a day spa."

When she didn't move, the retired military officer jumped off the park bench she'd been barking orders from and stormed toward her. Puffs of smoke from Captain Heather Moore's breath hit the crisp January air and trailed behind her like a dragon's smoke. She knelt and lifted the fleece ear warmer covering Brandi's ear.

"Need some motivation?" she asked softly, so only Brandi could hear. Heather's voice hardened. "Then think about that no-show jerk leaving you standing at the altar. Remember how you felt when his mother informed you he'd eloped with another woman?"

Brandi's hands clenched into fists at her sides. Six months hadn't dulled the humiliation of her would-be groom whisking the stripper he'd been cheating on her with to a Las Vegas chapel—while Brandi waited for him at a Nashville church packed with well-wishers. It was the most mortifying moment of her thirty-four years, and everyone she knew had witnessed it.

Heather gave the mental sore spot another poke.

"Now he has the nerve to accept the honor of best man at *your* sister's wedding." She made a tsking sound. "And I'll bet he's bringing his busty new wife along."

Anger began a slow burn through Brandi's worn-out body, energizing her depleted limbs. When she'd learned her future brother-in-law wanted Wesley as his best man, for her sister's sake, she'd hidden her true feelings.

Now Heather's taunts had excavated the hidden rage from the depths of her subconscious and dumped it in the forefront of her mind.

"Getting mad, huh?"

Brandi shot the trainer a look she hoped scorched the smirk off her face, but Heather kept pushing.

"So what's that loser going to do when he sees you next month?"

"Eat his heart out," Brandi practically growled. Cradling the back of her head in her hands, she curled her midsection into the first of fifty sit-ups. She'd never been stick thin, but months of comforting herself with massive amounts of chocolate had her wearing a larger size.

Even worse, she'd used her savings—money she'd squirreled away for years on her modest schoolteacher salary—to reimburse her mother for expenses connected to the big, non-wedding instead of its intended purpose of financing her boutique.

Ignoring the burning in her abdominal muscles, she cranked out one last sit-up. No way did she want Wesley back. However, now that pride was all she had left, Brandi refused to let her ex or his new wife see her looking anything less than fabulous.

Heather led the class through a stretch routine to end the workout. Afterward, as the other students milled away, Brandi sat cross-legged on the ground. She glanced around the park, situated across the street from her condo building, too sore and exhausted to contemplate hauling herself to her feet just yet.

Falling temperatures had driven most of her neighbors indoors. Apart from their class, a die-hard jogger and two men playing a game of one-on-one on the basketball court, the small park was deserted.

Brandi zeroed in on the duo playing ball. They'd shed their jackets, and even at a distance, she could see their fit physiques moved with an awe-inspiring mix of power and athletic grace.

Her gaze dropped to her own body, which was a long way from her goal of "fabulous." She'd purchased this violet-colored fleece outfit to boost her spirits. Unfortunately, the neon-bright shade only accentuated her excess lumps, and she felt huge exercising next to her thin, black-clad classmates.

Brandi blew out a sigh to signal the end of her pity party. It didn't matter how many push-ups she had to bang out or salads she had to eat. In the five remaining weeks between now and Erin's wedding, she was going to get in the best shape of her life.

"You okay?" Heather extended her hand.

Brandi groaned as she grabbed a hold of it and staggered to her feet.

"I will be after a soak in a tub full of bubbles and a decent night's sleep." She swiped her hand across her backside to dust away the twigs and dead leaves clinging to her pants.

Hopefully, she could sleep. For the past few nights, she'd awakened to the strangest thing—*the overwhelming scent of chocolate.*

"Hope I didn't go overboard back there," Heather said as they trudged across the park. "I only said what I did to get those crunches out of you."

"Don't worry. I stopped hating you by the time we started stretching."

Brandi had made the trainer well aware of her objective and the reason behind it when she'd enrolled in the class last week. In return, Heather had vowed to do everything in her power to help her reach her goal.

"That's good to know," Heather chuckled. "And by the way, you're doing great."

Brandi rolled her eyes. "You're kidding, right?"

"You made it through your third session. I had four students drop out after the first class and another…"

Heather's voice drifted off and Brandi followed her gaze to the two men she'd spotted earlier on the basketball court still embroiled in their game.

"Check out the eye candy." The trainer sighed. "Talk about yum!"

Brandi took in the view from the closer vantage point. Heather's description was no exaggeration. Both men stood well over six feet tall, and their perspiration-soaked T-shirts clung to wide shoulders, broad chests and impressively flat abs.

However, it was the one with the dark skin that captured Brandi's undivided attention and held on tight. His deep, rich complexion reminded her of the exquisite, midnight chocolate truffles she'd binged on over the past months, and she couldn't help wondering if he tasted as wickedly delicious.

Unconsciously, Brandi licked her lips.

As if he'd read her mind, the dark chocolate hunk stopped playing and turned in their direction. His handsome face broke into a wide smile that made her toes curl inside her sneakers.

"Mmm. I believe I've suddenly developed a sweet tooth." Heather shot her an elbow to the ribs. "What about you?"

Fortunately, Brandi's common sense snapped her out of her stupor at the same time the other man spoke to Mr. Dark Chocolate. He turned away.

"I've given up candy, remember?" Brandi resumed walking. She needed to stand around leering at a man like she needed a ten-pound box of Godiva's finest on her hips.

Heather rolled her eyes. "Come on, you know what kind of sweet stuff I'm talking about. I didn't work you *that* hard."

"Just because it looks or tastes good doesn't mean I have to have it," Brandi said. "I've learned my lesson."

"What are we talking about here, chocolate or men?"

"Both," Brandi said emphatically.

Adam Ellison couldn't keep his head in the game.

"We both know I'm going to win, but you normally put

up a decent fight." His brother, Kyle, dribbled the basket-ball, skirted around Adam and took a shot.

The ball sailed through the air in a perfect arc and swished unopposed through the hoop.

"That's game," the former college-star point guard crowed.

Adam knew his play hadn't been up to his usual stan-dard. He'd mentally checked out of their weekly one-on-one match over an hour ago. Since then, he'd blown easy baskets and let Kyle get away with moves he normally would have challenged with aggressive blocks and hard fouls.

His brother surveyed the pocket park near Adam's condo and frowned. "I can't believe I let you bully me into coming across town to this concrete playground, when there are perfectly good indoor courts at the club and our estate."

"Quit whining, man. It won't kill you to pull the silver spoon out of your behind once in a while," Adam said ab-sently, his mind still hung up on the purple-clad beauty who'd sashayed past them earlier.

All long legs and killer curves, Adam's mouth ran dry at the not-so-distant memory etched on his brain.

Mon Dieu! It had been a long time since he'd seen a woman who wasn't afraid to look like one. In a backward culture that glorified the skeletal and the surgically en-hanced, this lush knockout was a throwback to the days when voluptuous beauties like Pam Grier dominated the movie box office and black men's fantasies.

Even from a distance, he could see her flawless com-plexion was reminiscent of the creamy cappuccinos served in his favorite Parisian café. The thought of it brought a smile to his lips.

"What has you so off your game today?" Kyle backed

up and began shooting baskets from the free-throw line. "Regrets, maybe?"

He was having regrets all right, Adam conceded, but not the ones his brother hoped. Instead of standing there gawking like an idiot, he should have asked her out on the spot.

"I wouldn't blame you if you did," Kyle continued. "If I'd have tossed my job, a multimillion-dollar inheritance and a woman as rich as Jade Brooks away with one rash decision, I'd be kicking my own ass, too."

Adam let the comment slide. He knew where his brother wanted to steer this conversation, and he didn't want to go there.

"It's not too late to straighten this all out and get your old life back," Kyle pressed.

Although their game was over, Adam stole the ball and went in for a layup. "I don't want it back," he said, lunging for the basket.

"Get out of here with that weak shot." His brother leaped above the rim and slapped the ball out of bounds. He returned the conversation to the topic at hand. "Why the hell not?"

"Because I need more."

Adam wasn't surprised by the incredulous look on his brother's face.

"More what?" Kyle asked, as if he couldn't believe what he was hearing. "The combination of your job, inheritance and marrying into the Brooks Brand fortune would have made you a billionaire by age forty."

And end up like their father, Adam thought, slumped over dead at his desk with no one to grieve but a room full of indifferent business associates, a brother and two sons he rarely acknowledged outside of their role as vice presidents of the company he created.

"I'm doing okay financially," Adam said aloud.

Actually, better than okay. He'd invested his hefty salary wisely during his decade-long tenure as a vice president of Ellison Industries, the household-goods conglomerate founded by their late father, and was presently a millionaire in his own right. Now at thirty-five years old, he could live quite comfortably, even lavishly, without their family fortune.

Kyle retrieved the ball from the grass and took a shot. Despite the distance, Adam wasn't surprised to see it fall into the basket. The two of them may have been roughly the same size and build, but Kyle's legs turned into springs the moment a basketball was placed in his hands.

"What about Jade? You're just going to let her go?"

"She dumped me," Adam reminded him. She did so immediately after he'd told her of his decision to leave his position at Ellison Industries.

Kyle threw the ball to Adam. "Dad was looking forward to you two setting a date. It was all he talked about."

Months ago, his father's enthusiastic approval would have been reason enough for Adam to spend his life with Jade and continue to adhere to the blueprint the elder Ellison had outlined for his firstborn son's life.

Not anymore. Adam bounced the ball twice and hit a basket that would have been worth three points in a game. His priorities had shifted considerably since he'd been the one to find his father dead in his office.

Now Adam wanted more out of life than a job he didn't love and a woman who didn't love him.

"Jade's a good fit into our family," Kyle continued.

Grabbing the jackets they'd thrown on the ground earlier, Adam tossed one to his brother. Although they had different mothers, his father marrying Kyle's mother a few years after Adam's mother had died, they'd always been close. He didn't want this difference of opinion to cause a rift between them, but he wouldn't be manipulated.

His brother had more to say, but Adam forestalled him with a raised hand. "Tell Uncle Jonathan it won't work. Using a gotcha clause in Dad's will to screw with my inheritance didn't change my mind and having you try to play on my emotions won't, either."

Kyle shrugged on a hooded sweatshirt and seated himself on the backrest of the park bench next to the court. "Come on, man," he said. "Uncle Jon is only trying to do what Dad would have wanted. You back with Jade and at Ellison Industries."

"This is my life. Not Dad's."

Kyle scrubbed a hand down his face. "So you're flushing your life down the tubes over a *bake-off*."

Adam had explained it to his brother already, but Kyle, like their father and uncle, couldn't imagine anyone having an aspiration that was about their passion, not making more millions for Ellison Industries.

"I wouldn't exactly call the International Chocolate Pastry Competition a bake-off, but yes, it's important to me."

"For God's sake, why?"

Adam exhaled a weary sigh. "Haven't you ever wanted to achieve something on your own, without the benefit of our status or money?"

"Hell, no," Kyle replied. "I love being rich."

"Well, I need to do this."

Initially, Adam had only skimmed the application his grandmother had emailed him for the renowned competition. She'd noted for the first time ever there was a concurrent competition for amateur chefs, but Adam had been embroiled in his duties at Ellison Industries.

The day after they'd buried his father, Adam had retrieved the application from his deleted emails. Last week, he'd traveled to Montreal for the North American round of the competition, where his twist on chocolate lava cake won the title, beating out entries from over a hundred amateur chefs from the U.S. as well as Canada and Mexico.

Now he faced the monumental task of creating two chocolate-based entries so decadent and delicious, that he'd win the world title for self-taught chefs.

"But you already won first place for some pie, right?" Kyle asked.

"Cake," Adam corrected, knowing full well his brother couldn't care less.

Kyle hadn't spent summers and school holidays in Paris with maternal grandparents who owned a patisserie. So he hadn't grown up longing to follow in the footsteps of a grandfather who created the most magnificent chocolate pastries in the city.

"Whatever." Kyle tossed the ball in the air and caught it. "You've proved your point. Now it's time to get back to real life."

"The only thing I'm going back to is my kitchen," Adam said.

Scant weeks remained between now and the final rounds of the competition in Paris, and he still found his potential entries lacking. His focus had to remain on impressing an international jury of master pastry chefs. Not on his uncle, his ex or Ellison Industries.

And certainly not pursuing a purple-clad mystery woman.

A growl erupted from Brandi's stomach, the ferocious sound and accompanying hunger pangs waking her from a fitful sleep.

She inhaled deeply. As it had for the past week, the intoxicating aroma of chocolate surrounded her.

"Noooo."

She yanked the pillow from beneath her head and pulled it over her face to block out the scent and stop her mouth from watering. Who had moved into the place next door anyway, Betty Crocker?

The first night she'd thought it was simply a dream or better yet, a chocoholic dieter's hallucination. However, the night after she figured out the heavenly scent wasn't her subconscious balking against a menu of celery and frozen, low calorie meals.

It was chocolate all right, and her nose had pinpointed the source—the condo next door to hers.

Brandi had yet to spot her new neighbor, but the mid-night Mrs. Fields was wreaking havoc on her sleep and her willpower.

She tossed the pillow aside and glanced at the clock on her nightstand. *Who bakes at three o'clock in the morning?*

Her stomach roared again, making sleep out of the question.

Brandi kicked out from under the warmth of her blanket.

"Ow! Ow! Ow!" she chanted, her aching legs reminding her of the torture Heather had put them through. Easing her feet into slippers, she hobbled through her two-bedroom condo. Limping from the living room to the kitchen to the spare room she used as a studio for her online handbag boutique, there was no escaping the aroma that was turn-ing her knees to pudding. *Chocolate pudding.*

Sighing heavily, she slumped onto a stool in front of the breakfast bar. She stared longingly at the refrigerator until she remembered replacing the stash of chocolate bars in the vegetable crisper with actual vegetables.

"I'm not listening to you." She looked down at her rum-bling belly, noting the fumes now had her talking to herself.

Crossing the kitchen, she pulled a bowl of precut carrot and celery sticks from the fridge.

Unfortunately, the carrot did little to appease her appetite. In fact, the harder she chewed the crudités, the angrier she became.

Brandi crunched into a celery stick and thought about the day ahead. Ordinarily, she spent Saturdays in her sewing studio filling orders for her online boutique, Arm Candy. However, today she was meeting her sister and mother. Erin had already selected a wedding gown, and now it was time to pick a maid of honor dress for Brandi.

Truth be told, Brandi didn't wholeheartedly approve of her sister's upcoming nuptials to the Vanderbilt senior resident.

A nursing student at Tennessee State, Erin was book smart. However, she was also a young, spoiled and slightly immature twenty-two-year-old, and her fiancé was a bit too authoritative for Brandi's taste.

But when she'd tried to gently broach the subject with Erin or their mother, she was told unequivocally to mind her own business.

So the last thing she needed was to start her day off crabby and sleep deprived.

"It's not fair. I got rid of my chocolate stash so I wouldn't have to deal with temptation."

She inhaled deeply, and her stomach responded with a mournful noise that sounded like a wounded animal.

"Enough," Brandi announced. The way she saw it, her new neighbor had left her with one of two choices: either she suffered in silence every night or demanded whoever it was stop the chocolate torment.

Tossing the celery aside, she pulled her purple robe over her flannel pajamas and marched three feet down the corridor to the condo next to hers. She took a long, delicious breath in before raising her fist and banging on the door.

It swung open wide and Brandi cast her eyes on what was either her worst nightmare or most decadent fantasy.

Mr. Dark Chocolate from the park filled the door frame holding what she could only describe as *sex on a plate*.

Chapter 2

Shock held Brandi in a vise grip as her astonished gaze met his. He recovered first, and she watched his surprised expression melt into one of the sexiest smiles she'd ever encountered.

Her gaze skimmed his smooth dark skin, taking in the full lips and shadow of beard dusting his square jaw. A single word popped into her head.

Magnificent.

Despite the hour, her knock didn't appear to have awakened him. Jeans rode low on his lean hips and a black pullover sweater stretched across his broad chest.

"Do you like chocolate?" His deep baritone rumbled through her.

Breathe. Brandi gave herself a mental slap on the back.

"Uh…sure," she finally stammered.

"Then your visit is perfect timing."

She lowered her gaze to the sumptuous torte on the

plate in his hands and looked on mesmerized as he used the side of a fork to cut into it. He speared the morsel and held it out to her.

No way was this real, Brandi thought. Sexy strangers bearing chocolate were in the same category as the Easter Bunny and cute shoes left in her size at a fifty-percent-off sale. They flat-out didn't exist.

She slid her fingers up her arm to test the theory with a pinch, but stopped herself. If this was indeed a dream, did she really want to wake up?

Not yet, Brandi thought, as she leaned toward Mr. Dark Chocolate and wrapped her mouth around the fork.

Chocolate, laced with the complementary flavor of hazelnut, exploded on her tongue, and she couldn't help moaning aloud as she chewed.

"So what do you think?" he asked.

Think? There was no thinking in dreams. Besides, the exquisite hit of chocolate had stalled her brain along with her memory, and she promptly forgot the reason she'd knocked on his door in the first place.

"More," she demanded in a voice she didn't recognize as her own.

Brandi ate the second proffered bite with the same relish as the first. "Mmmm," she crooned. The smell and flavor made her feel like she was in Europe's finest bakery instead of her building's corridor.

"Wait here, I'll be right back." He ducked back inside with the torte and returned a millisecond later with a cake just as impressive.

"Try this one," he said, holding out a fork. "I've been experimenting with the recipe and could use some feedback."

"Look, I only came over to…"

"Please." He cut her off with what her mother used to call the magic word. However, on his lips it brought to mind carnal acts good mamas cautioned their daughters against unless they were in possession of a marriage license.

Brandi sighed and took the fork. Just one more bite, and that's it.

He held the plate while she dug into a cake so beautiful it belonged behind the glass case of an upscale bakery. "Oh, my God," she said, the taste rocking her world. "The first one was very, very good, but this is incredible."

Her enthusiasm was rewarded with another sexy, male smile, reminding her chocolate wasn't the only thing she'd been denying herself these days.

"I agree. The second is the better of the two," he said, leaning against the doorway. "But it's just not there yet."

"What's wrong with it?" Brandi asked, amazed anyone could find fault in either dessert.

"The balance of sweetness and chocolate is still slightly off."

On impulse, Brandi took another forkful of cake. This time she moved it slowly around her mouth giving her taste buds the opportunity to pick up all the flavors. She was by no means a chocolate connoisseur, but she'd eaten enough of the stuff to feel like one.

"I taste the milk chocolate, and both the white and dark chocolate," she said.

He nodded. "I've cut back on the sugar and experimented with the cacao content of the dark chocolate. While this is the best version so far, I'm still not totally pleased with it."

"As wonderful as this tastes, I wonder…" Brandi began as an idea formed in her head. "Since you're tinkering with the recipe, anyway…"

"Go on." He nodded eagerly.

"Well, I was thinking maybe you could add a pinch of

espresso to the bittersweet chocolate in the ganache. It might keep the sweetness in check and bring out the intensity of the chocolate." She shrugged. "Just a thought."

Adam appeared to mull the idea over in his head. "I'll give it a try and see what happens," he said, then added,"You certainly seem to know your chocolate."

Brandi snorted. "For the last six months, me and chocolate have been like this." She held up crossed fingers.

"So your visit really is perfect timing. I also made some pastries, and I'd love to get your opinion," he said. "Come inside."

Brandi took a step toward his threshold. Then her brain kicked into gear, and she stopped in her tracks.

What in the hell was she doing?

Getting sidetracked from her diet was one thing, following a stranger into his place was another. She squared her shoulders and cleared her throat. "As I was saying, I live next door…"

"Adam Ellison. I moved in a few days ago," he said smoothly as if it were three in the afternoon instead of in the morning.

"Brandi Collins," she said. "Anyway, I need to talk to you about…"

He sniffed. "Damn!"

Shoving the cake into her hands, he dashed inside.

"But I'm not supposed to eat chocolate," she said. However, it was too late, he was already out of earshot.

"Come on in," he called back.

Brandi stepped into the entryway. She'd simply hand him back his plate of triple chocolate yumminess, say her piece and be on her way, she reasoned as she followed the sound of his footsteps echoing against the hardwood floor.

She glanced at the living area as she passed. Only a huge flat-screen television, tuned in to the twenty-four-hour sports channel, and easy chair occupied the otherwise empty space. Brandi quickly did the math in her head. A sparse man cave of a living room plus zero dining-room furniture added up to a very single Mr. Dark Chocolate.

She caught herself smiling at the thought and then quickly reminded herself his eligibility was none of her concern.

Mr. Dark Chocolate was pulling a round cake pan from the top portion of a double-wall oven when she walked into the kitchen. He frowned at the curl of smoke rising from the cake.

"That's probably my fault. Sorry if I distracted you, Mr. Dar…Ellison," she quickly corrected.

"No, I should have set the timer." He dumped the scorched cake into a trashcan. "And it's Adam."

Brandi glanced around the kitchen. If his living room screamed undomesticated bachelor, the kitchen was like stepping into the prep area of a gourmet restaurant.

Professional, stainless-steel appliances gleamed against a background of polished cherrywood cabinets and shiny hardwood floors. An overhead pot rack, in the same brushed nickel of the cabinet knobs and handles, hung above a massive kitchen island workstation.

Her gaze dropped to the island's granite countertop, and a gasp escaped her lips.

"Wow," she whispered, feeling like she just stepped into a cover shoot for a food magazine.

Brandi looked from a basket heaped with flaky, chocolate croissants to a tray of glossy, strawberry-topped chocolate tarts. Both looked too pretty to eat.

Adam inclined his head toward the bounty. "Help yourself."

Brandi stared at the treats, resisting the urge to snatch up the biggest croissant and stuff it into her mouth like a greedy toddler. She shook her head. "No, thanks. I'm not hungry."

Her stomach took the opportunity to counteract her statement with a loud wail of protest. Brandi cringed as she watched the corner of Adam's mouth twitch upward.

"Are you sure?" he asked.

Her resolve wavering, Brandi summoned up her trainer's motivational speech from earlier to bolster the little resistance she had left.

"...think about that no-show jerk leaving you standing at the altar. Remember how you felt when his mother informed you he'd eloped the night before with another woman?"

However, instead of the anger it had evoked before, she found herself comparing her neighbor to her ex-fiancé.

Where Wesley's body had begun to grow pudgy from too many sedentary hours behind a desk at the business magazine he edited, Adam Ellison was obviously no stranger to the gym. His sweater couldn't disguise the hard, sculpted torso and bulging biceps she'd glimpsed earlier at the park.

Wesley had never bothered to make coffee. Yet, within seconds of meeting him this man had practically handfed her.

Whoa! Brandi stomped the brakes on her runaway thoughts. Her new neighbor had already invaded her condo with his chocolate. She didn't need him taking up space in her head.

She set the cake she was still holding on the countertop and took a step backward to put physical distance between her, the man and his culinary offerings.

Brandi cleared her throat. "I didn't come here to eat. I came to ask you to stop."

"Stop what?" Concern radiated in his dark brown eyes.

"All of this." She spread her arms, gesturing toward the pastry-laden countertop with a frustrated wave. Brandi knew she sounded as deranged as she must look standing there in her pajamas in the middle of the night, but she was here now, and it was past time for her to put an end to the chocolate torture.

"I need you to shut down the all-night chocolate buffet."

Adam had envisioned a few scenarios if he ever encountered the beauty from the park again. Most of them involved her in his bed. None of them included her standing in the middle of his kitchen ranting about chocolate.

"Why?" he asked. "Does the building have a covenant or restriction on baking at night that I missed?"

Brandi shook her head. "Nothing like that."

Even if they did, Adam didn't have time to scrounge around for another kitchen space with the final round of the competition only a few weeks away.

The transition from his family's sprawling estate to this condo which he'd purchased years ago as an investment property, had eaten up enough valuable baking time. But the move had been necessary. His new home provided the solitude he needed to perfect his entries without distractions or interference.

"Then there's no reason for me to stop."

He opened the small, leather-bound notebook, similar to the moleskin one his grandfather had used to record recipes and notes, and began jotting down possible changes to the cake recipe. He silently debated whether to tweak the current or an earlier version of the triple chocolate dessert that included pistachios.

"I can't deal with this aroma every night. I'm trying to lose…" Brandi paused. "Are you even listening to me?"

"Of course. Your suggestion was to add espresso to the bittersweet chocolate, right?"

"Yes," she said. "But as I was saying, I'm trying to lose weight."

Adam looked up from the notebook. "Mind if I ask why?"

"My sister's getting married next month, and I need to look my best for the wedding."

He closed the notebook, and his gaze slid from her face downward to the heavy robe and flannel pajamas his neighbor apparently wore to bed. If she were his, he thought, the nights they shared would be too hot for flannel. *Or anything else.*

"You mean you want to be skinny, because you're already the best-looking woman I've seen in a very long time."

Her eyes widened and her pretty face flushed with color. The guileless reaction instantly endeared her to him. It also told him she hadn't been told what a knockout she was nearly often enough.

Brandi cleared her throat. "That's very flattering, but I still have a goal to meet," she said. "And the smells coming from your place are driving me bonkers. Look at me, I'm standing here in my pj's at three in the morning practically begging you to turn your oven off."

"Smells that good, huh?" Adam couldn't suppress the big grin spreading across his face.

She frowned. "Better."

Adam was exhausted. He'd initially planned to hold off making another cake, incorporating Brandi's suggestions, until after he got some rest. However, the knowledge his baking had such an overwhelming effect on her instantly revitalized him. He stepped over to the walk-in pantry and retrieved a clean, bibbed apron from the hook inside. He pulled it over his head and washed his hands at the sink.

"What are you doing?" Brandi asked.

Adam retrieved two cake pans and deftly coated them with butter and a dusting of flour.

"Making a cake." He pulled a roll of parchment paper from a drawer. "Have a seat. I'm sure you'll want to taste the results of your suggestions."

When he looked up, Brandi was still standing and she didn't look pleased.

"The whole point of my coming here was to get you to stop."

"Can't do that." He began assembling ingredients on the kitchen island countertop.

"Why not?" She paused and looked around. "Come to think of it, why are you up at this time of night cooking, anyway?"

"I'm preparing for a competition."

"What kind of…?" She bumped her forehead with the heel of her hand. "Of course, it has to be a chocolate competition."

Adam nodded. "More like the mother of all chocolate competitions. Pastry chefs come from all over to compete in the International Chocolate Pastry Competition."

"So you're a pastry chef?"

"Amateur." He unwrapped a block of chocolate, placed it on a dry cutting board and began chopping it into small chunks with the edge of a serrated knife. "But last week I managed to win a chocolate pastry competition, and now I'm preparing to represent North America in the international event."

"If the smells coming out of here are any indication, I'm not surprised you won." Brandi's eyes flitted back to the croissants and tarts. "Still, weren't you intimidated by all those chefs with culinary degrees and years of experience?"

Adam shrugged. "I compete in the self-taught chef division, so I'm on somewhat equal footing with everyone else. Anyway, the competition was sort of a lark, and I didn't think much about the competing aspect. I was just happy to be there."

"And now?"

It means everything, Adam thought. "I quit my job to focus on the international competition, which pissed off just about everyone I know." He measured out sugar, cocoa and an assortment of other ingredients and dumped them into a metal mixing bowl. "So I have a lot riding on the outcome."

In the short silence, Adam reviewed the rewards of the competition. The grand prize for the winner of the amateur chef division included full-color spreads in both *Gourmet* and *Cuisine et Vins de France* magazines, a guest appearance as a judge on a Food Network dessert competition show and two hundred and fifty thousand dollars in business start-up money.

While he could have easily pulled the money from one of his accounts, the prestige and exposure that came along with the other prizes were invaluable.

"I think it's a gutsy move," Brandi said.

Adam did a double take, not quite believing his ears. He'd heard his decision of late described in many ways. This had been the first favorable one he'd heard from someone besides his grandmother.

"Then you're definitely in the minority." He placed the metal bowl underneath a stainless-steel stand mixer and turned it on a low setting.

"So what was your old career?"

Adam hesitated a moment, silently debating how much

to reveal. It appeared Ellison was just another surname to her. She hadn't mentioned awareness of the parent company of the popular brands of detergent, dish soap and paper towels she used in her everyday life, and Adam wanted to keep it that way, at least for now.

"I worked for a household-goods company."

Brandi wrinkled her nose. "Sounds dull. No wonder you quit," she said. "How'd you get stuck in that job?"

Adam threw his head back and laughed. Her honesty was as fresh as her beauty. She also managed to sum up in one word how he'd felt each morning he'd donned a suit and tie and headed to work to pursue his father's dream for him. *Stuck.*

"Long story short, it was chosen for me." He braced his hands on the countertop. "How about you? What do you do for a living?"

"High school teacher."

"Enjoy it?"

She shrugged. "I'm good at it, and I love the kids."

He raised a brow. "That doesn't answer my question."

"Like you, it's a long story, but let's just say it wasn't my first choice of career."

Adam was curious, but didn't press. He was going to enjoy getting to know his neighbor. This place was turning out to be an even better investment than he'd thought.

A growl sounded, again coming from the direction of Brandi's stomach. He looked across the kitchen island at her and followed her gaze to the tarts and croissants he'd made earlier.

"You realize how ridiculous you're being, right?"

She abruptly turned away from the pastries. The expression on her face reminded him of a kid caught with a hand elbow-deep in the cookie jar.

"I don't know what you're talking about."

Her stomach rumbled noisily, and he raised a brow. "Oh, I think you do," he said. "I also think it's silly for you to refuse food you obviously want and you're more than welcome to enjoy."

Her mouth tightened. "I already told you…"

"Yes, I know." Adam checked the cake batter. "You're starving yourself for your sister's wedding."

"Which brings me back to the reason I knocked on your door in the first place. I'm hoping we could find some kind of middle ground."

"I don't think there is one," he said. "Until I perfect my entries, I expect to be working on them day and night."

"Then my coming here was a total waste of time."

Brandi's frown morphed into a full-out scowl, and Adam realized his chances of getting her to go out with him were nil. He switched off the mixer. This was probably the last time she'd talk to him anyway, so he had nothing to lose by telling her exactly what he thought.

"The truth is I wouldn't help you even if I could. It's refreshing to see a shapely woman with an hourglass figure. Frankly, I wouldn't lift a finger to help you to minimize a body I can't keep my eyes off."

Her mouth fell open, and her brown eyes narrowed, suspicion glinting in their depths. "So what are you, one of those chubby chasers like on that TV reality show?"

Adam paused for a moment trying to figure out what she was talking about, and then realization dawned. He threw his head back and laughed.

"No." He shook his head, still laughing. "I'm just a normal guy who appreciates a woman with a few well-placed curves."

Adam walked around the kitchen island where Brandi stood and sat on one of the stools she'd refused. He picked up the flakiest, most chocolate-infused croissant off the pile. The very one he knew she'd been ogling.

"I also hate to see you deprive yourself of something I'd be delighted to give you."

Brandi continued to glare at him. Then her gaze fell to the croissant and she licked her lips.

"No, thanks," she said, but he could feel her resolve wavering.

"Come on, join me," he coaxed, patting the stool beside him with his other hand. "Stop trying to resist the irresistible."

Her back stiffened. "Oh, I can resist, all right," she said. "Just watch me."

Adam watched as she spun on the heel of her slipper and made her exit.

He took a bite out of the croissant and chewed. It was for the best, he told himself. His focus needed to be on the competition, not kissing that sexy mouth of hers until he made her moan for him the way she had over his chocolate.

Chapter 3

Brandi stifled a yawn with her fist.

"Are we boring you?"

"Of course not, Mom." She silently cursed Adam for keeping her up all night. Thanks to him, she'd been forced to endure an entire morning of shopping with her mother and sister on nearly zero sleep.

It had been a mistake to go next door, Brandi fumed. A chocolate-scented condo was bad enough. Now she had to deal with the knowledge that only a thin wall separated her from the sexiest man she'd ever laid eyes on.

"Stop trying to resist the irresistible."

His deep voice echoed in her head while an imagination-fueled vision of him feeding her chocolate played through her mind. In her fantasy, she didn't attempt to resist, and sweets weren't all he was offering.

"Brandi!"

Jolene Collins's voice yanked her away from the

chocolate-dipped-strawberries-with-her-nearly-naked-neighbor fantasy back to reality. "Stand up straight and spin around so we can see how this one looks on you."

Brandi winced at her mother's annoyed tone. She indeed deserved it and the disapproving frown, but for a different reason than her mom intended. She should be thinking up ways to avoid the man next door, not casting him as the leading man of her daydreams.

She turned slowly on the raised platform, while her mother and sister sat on the bridal salon's floral armchairs scrutinizing the fit of yet another dress. Brandi averted her eyes from the three-way mirror as she rotated, not needing her reflection to confirm how absurd she looked squeezed into the red sequined mermaid-style dress. Not to mention the humongous bow riding her ample bottom.

Her mother was impeccably outfitted in a gray sweaterdress and matching suede boots that made her appear a decade younger than her sixty years. She leaned forward in her chair and surveyed Brandi, before exchanging a sidelong glance with Erin.

"Reject pile?"

Her sister nodded and turned to the beleaguered salon attendant, who scurried off for more dresses.

"I don't know, Mom," Erin whined. "Ashley, Taylor and Tiffany are still really upset about not being bridesmaids, and they're my best friends."

Jolene patted her youngest daughter's hand, and a pang of longing lodged in Brandi's chest. She'd always envied their special mother-daughter bond. Brandi tried to be good to her mother, but they'd grown apart in the years since Brandi's father died.

Like Jolene Collins, Erin was petite and pretty, and together they were a striking pair. Next to them, Brandi, who favored her late father's side of the family, felt like an elephant clomping alongside two swans.

"We've already been over this, honey. You and Maurice only got engaged on Christmas Eve and expect me to pull together a decent wedding by Valentine's Day, *this* Valentine's Day. No wedding planner would take on the job, and I barely have time to plan as it is. There isn't time to corral a bunch of bridesmaids into fittings and such."

"Yeah, I know." Erin sighed.

"I tried to convince you to wait until summer," their mother said. "You'll have your nursing degree and Maurice would be done with his residency."

Erin shook her head. "Everybody gets married during the summer. I want a Valentine's Day wedding."

"Well then, you'll just have to settle for your sister as maid of honor."

Brandi stepped down from the platform and inched her way toward the dressing room's changing cubicle, her movements restricted by the tight-fitting gown.

"This is a disaster," Erin said after Brandi was behind the cubicle door and presumably out of earshot. "All of the cute dresses look horrendous on her. Brandi's wedding was a hot mess. Now she's going to ruin mine."

Unfortunately, Erin was terrible at whispering. So was their mother.

"Lord knows she was all boobs and behind before, but since Wesley took off…" her mother said.

"She must have gained at least thirty pounds," Erin hissed. *Twenty,* Brandi silently corrected, wishing the dressing room had an escape hatch.

Brandi pushed open the cubicle door and walked back out to the mirrored area. "I don't want to spoil this for you," she told her baby sister. "You can ask one of your girlfriends to stand in as your maid of honor. I'll be happy to sit with the guests while you and Maurice exchange vows."

Erin's eyes lit up. "You'd really do that for me?"

"Of course not," their mother interjected. "Don't be ridiculous, Brandi. How would it look if you weren't in your own sister's wedding? After your fiasco, I refuse to be publically humiliated again. I've only recently been able to show my face at my women's club meetings. *This wedding* has to be perfect."

The rustle of fabric signaled the attendant's return, putting an end to the debate.

"I know you specified all-over sequins, but I took the liberty of bringing another style for your sister to try," the attendant told Erin. "It's a compromise, but should give you the look you want for your maid of honor as well as flatter her curves."

"But I want…" Erin started to protest.

"Let her try it on, sweetheart." Their mother cut her off. "This is the third shop we've been to, and we have several other appointments scheduled for this afternoon."

"I don't know, Mom," Erin hedged.

"Valentine's Day is just five weeks away. We don't have a moment to waste."

"Oh, all right," Erin relented.

Brandi took the red dress from the attendant and headed back to the dressing cubicle. She slid the zipper down the side of the sequined bodice and slipped it over her head. A sigh of relief escaped her lips when the chiffon skirt slid easily over her hips and thighs.

She tugged the zipper upward before it caught at the halfway mark. A glance in the mirror revealed an inch-wide gap of skin stood between the zipper's teeth.

"What's taking you so long? Don't tell me this one doesn't fit, either." Her mother tried to push open the cubicle door, but fortunately Brandi had had the foresight to latch it. "We don't have all day. Your sister has an appointment with the baker this afternoon."

"Come on," Brandi begged, tugging at the zipper.

Holding her breath, she gave it one last yank and mouthed a silent prayer when it finally closed. It was a snug fit, but the style was more forgiving than the others she'd tried on.

She opened the cubicle door to find her mother standing in front of it with her arms crossed. "What on earth possessed you to lock the door? There's nobody here but family."

That's exactly why, Brandi thought. "Sorry," she said aloud.

"Well, let's see what you look like," Jolene said.

Brandi stepped up on the raised platform and ventured a peek at the mirror. Amazingly, the sequined, strapless bodice flattered her generous bustline.

Not bad, she thought, double-checking the flanking mirrors. An empire waistline gave the illusion of a narrow waist before the dress released into a swirly skirt.

"Ahhh, this style is much better on you," the attendant said. "You look beautiful."

Brandi thanked her before glancing over at her mother and sister.

Her youngest sister gasped at the sight of her and her face broke out in a grin. "That's it! We've finally found the dress. What do you think, Mom?"

Their mother's eyes narrowed as she scrutinized her from head to toe. "It looks a little tight to me." Jolene stepped up on the platform and tugged at the dress's ruched waistband. "Can you breathe?"

"It's fine, Mom," Brandi said.

"I don't know, Erin. Looks to me like she needs to size

up." Their mother ignored Brandi's protest. "It's a close fit at best, and I expect in the weeks before the wedding, she'll only get bigger."

Erin flashed Brandi an apologetic look. "Just to be on the safe side," she said.

"I'll just pull one in the next size up for her to try on," the attendant said.

"Make that two sizes bigger," Jolene added. "I don't want any last-minute snafus."

"No, wait!" Brandi called out before she could stop herself.

Conversation halted, and the attendant stopped mid-step. Brandi watched as three pairs of eyes fixed upon her.

"A larger size won't be necessary," she said. "I'm on a diet, and I've enrolled in an exercise class. In a few weeks, I'll be wearing a smaller size, not larger."

"Hmm." Jolene's lips remained pursed.

"It's a boot camp class," Brandi explained. "It's only been a week, and I'm sore all over, but I'm determined to get this extra weight off."

Her mother looked unimpressed. "It's nice that you're trying, dear, but you do realize the wedding is just five weeks away."

Brandi nodded. "I do, and I'm still buying this dress."

Jolene rolled her eyes heavenward and sighed. "Okay, but I'm going to pay for one in the larger size myself, just in case…" Her voice trailed off, but the unspoken "you fail" echoed in Brandi's head.

Her mother had better save the receipt, Brandi vowed, because there was no way she could fail now.

Adam slowed his pace to a walk as the treadmill shifted into cool-down mode, winding up his five-mile run. He swiped at the sweat on his brow with his forearm and glanced around the country-club gym.

"Where is he?" Adam muttered.

His friend Zeke Holden had been a no-show for their standing tennis game. Their court time was for over an hour ago and once again, he hadn't emailed or left a message saying he wouldn't be able to make it.

Adam pulled his phone, which did double duty as his mp3 player, from the pouch on his arm. It rang twice before bouncing him to Zeke's voice mail, like it had the last few times he'd called.

"Hey man, I thought you were eager to get some revenge for the beat down I gave you last time. Hope everything is okay with you. Give me a call."

He and Zeke had been friends since they were kids, both having the pressure of growing up in the shadow of their successful businessman fathers.

On the other hand, Kyle and Zeke had never gotten along. His brother didn't like Zeke and trusted him even less.

The treadmill belt slowed to a halt and the console flashed his workout stats. Adam made a mental note to drive out to his friend's place if he didn't hear from him soon.

First, this evening, he had another visit to pay.

Images of Brandi Collins sprang to mind as he walked to the locker room to shower and dress. After she'd stormed out of his condo, he'd made the cake incorporating her suggestions, and the result had been pure perfection. Thanks to her, he'd solidified his first entry for the competition.

Ecstatic, his first inclination had been to go next door and literally serve it to her on a silver platter. But after the way they'd left things, he was sure his was the last face she'd want to see.

Adam sighed. He would have to remedy that, because he needed his curvy new neighbor's help.

Twenty minutes later, thoughts of her lingered as he made a detour to the club's grille for a sandwich to go before heading home. He seated himself at the bar with a bottled water to wait for the staff to prepare his order. A Nashville Predators game blared on the television, but Adam ignored the hockey match. He had a tricky negotiation ahead, and despite an MBA and decade of executive experience, he was at a loss.

What could he possibly say to convince Brandi to jeopardize her goal *for his?*

A familiar voice interrupted his thoughts.

"Well, if it isn't the prodigal nephew."

"Uncle Jonathan," Adam said in way of acknowledgment. He hadn't seen much of his uncle in the weeks since the blowup over his resignation and subsequent breakup with Jade. Adam had tried talking to him, but each attempt deteriorated into an argument.

"I'm surprised to see you here." His uncle's second chin wobbled as he spoke, a testament to his eschewing the club's courts, gym and Olympic-sized pool in favor of the two five-star restaurants and walk-in cigar humidor. Though he was outfitted in athletic wear, it was clear the only sweating he did was in the club's steam room. "I thought you'd thumbed your nose at the good life."

"Like you, I hold a lifetime membership in this club," Adam said.

His uncle hefted his bulk onto the bar stool next to him, and Adam's hopes of using this time to figure out an approach to the Brandi dilemma evaporated.

"Give me a scotch, neat." The elder Ellison directed the bartender and then swiveled in his seat toward Adam. "We need to talk."

"About what?" They were at an impasse, and if his uncle's demeanor was any indication, the chances of this conversation ending in reconciliation were slim.

"What's it going to take to get you back behind your desk at Ellison and down the aisle with Jade Brooks?"

Adam shook his head. "Not going to happen."

His uncle pressed on as if he hadn't heard Adam's reply. "I've been in touch with Jade's family, and the Brookses are willing to overlook your temporary lapse in judgment," he said. "They understand you weren't thinking clearly after your father's death. We'd all like to move forward and put this unpleasantness behind us."

"My lapse, as you call it, is permanent, Uncle Jonathan. Your time would be better spent on something other than my personal life."

Jonathan Ellison took a sip of his drink. "You're my brother's firstborn and with him not here, your personal life is my business."

"Business being the operative word, right?" Adam snorted. "Don't insult my intelligence by pretending to care about me and Jade's relationship."

His uncle shrugged. "Jade Brooks is an attractive young woman. You could do a lot worse."

"All any of you *really* care about is merging Ellison with Brooks Brand and sealing the deal with a marriage."

His uncle jabbed a fat finger in his direction. "Don't get all sanctimonious with me. You sat in on those meetings with your father and old man Brooks. You know damn well what this was all about as well as what's at stake."

Adam nodded. "You're absolutely right."

He watched a smug smile spread across the elder Ellison's lips. "So you're going to straighten things out with Jade?"

"No. I mean you're right in that I sold my soul for a business deal," he said. "But now I'm reclaiming it. No deal."

Angry eyes the same shade of brown as his father's stared back at him. "Thank goodness my brother had the foresight to add those stipulations to his will," he said. "Until Ellison Industries and Brooks Brand are one, and we're all a big happy family, you can forget about seeing one dime of your inheritance."

"I can live with that," Adam said.

"But can you live with flushing your father's big plans for you and Ellison Industries down the toilet?"

His uncle's criticism stung. Adam reminded himself he'd been a good son to David Ellison and had dedicated the majority of his life to pleasing him.

It was time he pleased himself.

"I have my own plans."

"You mean the pastry chef nonsense." His uncle took a gulp of his drink. "I thought David drummed that notion out of your head when you were a kid."

The bartender brought Adam's take-out bag to the bar. He rose from his seat and retrieved his wallet from his back pocket. He dropped a bill on the table large enough to cover it and his uncle's drink.

"We're done here." Adam picked up the food for which he no longer had an appetite. "Enjoy your drink, uncle. It's on me."

"We'll see how far your so-called plans go without Ellison clout and cash to back them up," his uncle called after him. "You'll come crawling back after you make a mess of everything, and I can hardly wait to rub your nose in it."

Chapter 4

Brandi stitched the woven Arm Candy label to the inside of the newly completed handbag.

While the bulk of her sewing was done on the industrial machine and serger surrounding her on the U-shaped desk, she preferred adding this final touch to her creations by hand.

It wasn't the most scintillating way for a single woman to spend a Saturday night, but after a trying morning of shopping for her maid-of-honor dress with her mother and sister she relished spending the evening in her studio.

Brandi snipped the thread and held up the bag she'd dubbed the *City Girl Sling*. Customers who selected zebra print for the main exterior for their custom handbag usually opted for coordinating solid color for the band and strap. However, this customer had checked off the box on the online order form for a clashing cheetah print.

It wasn't her favorite look, but the point of a customized bag was to give her customers *their* favorite look.

The doorbell sounded, and she glanced at the face of her nearby phone. Eight o'clock.

"Who the…" she muttered at the interruption.

The bell buzzed again.

Brandi peered through the front door peephole expecting to see her mom, sister or perhaps her friend Lynn, but instead her new neighbor's face stared back at her.

Damn. What did he want?

It had taken hours to purge hot, sexy images she'd conjured up of Adam Ellison and his chocolate delights from her head. The last thing she needed was another encounter with him.

Smoothing her hair, she glanced down at her jeans and purple blouse. They were a lot crisper when she'd donned them this morning, but it was too late to change now.

"Oh, just find out what he wants and get rid of him," she mumbled. It wasn't like she was trying to make a good impression.

Blowing out a breath, she yanked open the door.

"Yes?" she inquired in a tone she hoped was rude enough to do the trick.

He flashed her the identical smile he wore in her daydreams, but in them it wasn't all he flashed.

"Good evening to you, too, neighbor."

Brandi leaned against the doorjamb and crossed her arms over her chest. "Don't tell me," she said. "You're here to force-feed me éclairs. Or maybe a macaroon?"

He dropped his head in a semblance of contrition. "I came to apologize for upsetting you earlier, but you're not going to make it easy on me, are you?"

"Why should I?"

"Because when I'm not strung out over this competition, I'm a decent guy." He pulled a bouquet of lavender roses from behind his back. "A peace offering."

Stunned by the gesture, Brandi straightened and pulled away from the door frame. She'd never seen a bouquet quite like it. Sure, her ex had given her flowers on Valentine's Day or her birthday, but they were always run-of-the-mill posies he'd grabbed at the last minute from the grocery store.

"I promise they're calorie free," Adam coaxed, extending the paper-wrapped bouquet toward her.

"Thank you. They're lovely," she said, taking the flowers. She pressed her nose against the petals and inhaled, then eyed him over the top of the massive bouquet. He wore dark wool slacks, and a white T-shirt peeked out from under the V-neck of his navy cashmere sweater. He looked good.

"Does this mean you're shutting down your chocolate factory, Mr. Ellison?" Brandi asked, after she managed to stop ogling him.

"It's Adam." He shook his head. "And no, I'll still have the place reeking with the stuff for the next month or so."

"Oh," Brandi said flatly.

Adam rallied. "But like the worn-out line politicians like to repeat, I'd hoped we could disagree without being disagreeable."

"We'll see." Brandi shrugged. It wasn't like the flowers had actually changed anything. He'd still be turning her place into a chocolate torture chamber, not to mention the deliciously wicked scenarios she was cooking up about him in her head.

Adam took a step forward, closing the gap between them. "Come on," he coaxed. "Let's be friends."

Fortunately, the roses provided a physical barrier between them and kept her from doing something stupid, like kissing those full lips to see if they felt as good as they looked. She swallowed hard.

"Other than the chocolate thing, you have to admit I'm a fantastic neighbor," he continued. "I don't blast hip-hop music. No yapping dog or screaming baby. I haven't *borrowed* your morning paper."

She chuckled. "Or swiped my parking space."

"Exactly," he said. "So the neighborly thing for you to do is invite me inside for coffee and see if we can't start our relationship off on better footing."

Blowing out a breath, Brandi beckoned him inside. The man lived right next door. She couldn't avoid him forever.

His broad shoulders spanned the entryway as he moved past her, and his delicious scent filled her nostrils. She felt her insides go all warm and gooey like the inside of a molten lava cake.

God, what was wrong with her? For months, she hadn't even thought about sex. Now a man she'd known for less than twenty-four hours had lit the pilot light under her dormant libido, and she couldn't think of anything else.

She cut a wide berth around the tower of boxes near the doorway filled with handbag orders ready to be shipped. "Have a seat while I put these in water and see about that coffee."

Thankfully, the minutes it took to arrange the roses in a vase and get the coffee started helped her gain perspective on her out-of-whack hormones.

Her so-called attraction to Adam was nothing more than a side effect of this godforsaken diet she was on. It probably wasn't even him she craved, Brandi reasoned. He just reminded her of chocolate.

Satisfied she'd successfully diagnosed her problem, Brandi joined her unexpected guest in the living room where he'd seated himself on the sofa. His tall, masculine body looked out of place on the dainty blush-pink piece of furniture.

Placing the flowers on the coffee table, Brandi sat down in the nearby accent chair. "The coffee will be ready in a few moments."

She watched him take in the creamy beige walls, hint-of-pink microsuede chairs and sofa, and leafy green plants. The strong, dark wood of her tables and polished hardwood floors took the girly edge off the pink.

"Nice place," he said.

"I thought so until I saw how much bigger yours is than mine," she said. "I'd assumed all of the condos in the building were the same size."

"I bought back when the building was still in the planning stages, so I was able to double up on the square footage. It was originally designated to be two units."

"Then you've always owned it?"

He nodded, which prompted her next question. "I've lived here for five years. How come I've never seen you until yesterday?"

"This was an investment property. I didn't plan on making it my home."

"Until you left your job," she said.

"Yes. So it turned out to be a good investment after all."

The coffeemaker gurgled, signaling the end of the brewing cycle.

"I'd better see to the coffee."

When she returned, carrying a tray bearing two mugs of coffee, cream and sugar, he was eyeing the stack of boxes by her front door. "Christmas present backlog?"

She turned to the pile and laughed. "They're orders for my business."

"What kind of business?"

With a small pause and a blush, Brandi explained. "I

make custom-designed handbags and sell them through my online store."

"Thought you were a teacher?"

She nodded. "I am a high school art teacher by day. At night, I shut myself in my home studio and transform into a designing diva."

He flashed her a smile, revealing straight white teeth and a rogue dimple in one cheek. "That's an impressive stack of boxes. You must be very good at it."

"I think so."

He inclined his head toward the boxes. "And you manage to do all of this here?"

She nodded. "I turned the master bedroom into a studio, and I sleep in the smaller one."

"Must be quite an operation."

"Would you like to see it?" The offer tumbled out of her mouth before she could get ahold of her tongue.

"Yeah, I would," Adam said, appearing genuinely interested.

Leaving the coffee untouched, they rose from their seats and Brandi led him to the room off the dining room.

She opened her arms with a grand air over the room she'd painted a vibrant shade of orange. Track lighting shone down on her sewing machines, cutting table and bolts of fabric.

"Welcome to Arm Candy Handbags," she said.

Looking on as he surveyed the heart of her business, Brandi wondered what had possessed her to invite him. Ordinarily, she kept the door closed to everyone except her friend and coworker, Lynn Myers, the computer tech teacher who'd built and maintained Arm Candy's website.

Maybe it was the brief kinship she'd felt toward him after he'd mentioned his new career direction had *pissed off everyone around him*. Brandi didn't have to imagine how the lack of support from those closest to him made him feel.

Adam walked over to the chrome shelves, which held an assortment of completed bags ready to be boxed and shipped. He picked up a tote in a turquoise honeycomb pattern with orange suede trim and handles. He examined it and then the blue-and-lime-floral shoulder bag next to it.

"Wow. These are amazing." He looked from the bags to her. "I had no idea I was living next door to such a talented woman."

"Thanks." Brandi beamed.

"I'm no connoisseur on women's purses, but these look like something you'd purchase at a swanky boutique."

"Now that you've seen the finished product, let me show you the process."

Brandi led him over to the laptop computer perched on her cutting table and pulled up her website. She felt the warmth emanating from his body as they stood over the screen.

"It begins here on Arm Candy's website," she said. Thankfully, her voice remained steady and didn't reveal the impact his nearness had on her. "It's interactive. Customers select a style of bag and then click through to make picks from the available fabrics for the exterior, interior, straps and trim."

"Can I give it a try?" Adam asked.

"Um, sure, but *you* want a handbag?"

"For my grandmother." Adam laughed. "I noticed a French market tote is one of your style options, and she'd love it."

Brandi guided him through the process. "Since you're here, I can actually show you the fabrics. The online swatches are great, but not as good as being able to see and touch the cloth yourself."

"Red is her favorite color," he said.

As Adam made his fabric selections on the computer, Brandi brought him a bolt of it to view. Ten minutes later, he'd decided on a bright red poppy print with black straps and handles.

Brandi saw him pull his credit card from his wallet and stopped him. "It's on me," she said. "Consider the cost a housewarming gift."

Adam shook his head. "That's not necessary," he said, continuing to input his card info into the website. "A lot of handiwork goes into these bags. You deserve to be compensated."

"As promised on the site, the bag should be ready in a few days. I hope your grandmother enjoys it."

"No rush to get it done," he said. "I want to give it to her in person, and I won't see her again until next month."

Brandi nodded and stepped away from him. Now that she'd demonstrated the website, there was no reason for them to stand quite so close. There was no need to continue allowing his warmth or his masculine scent to wreak havoc on her hormones.

"I appreciate your business."

Her move to put distance between them must not have been as discreet as she'd thought. He gave her a knowing smile and took a step toward her, closing it.

"This is quite an operation. Now I understand the number of boxes at your door."

"It's kept me busy."

He glanced around. "It looks like you're outgrowing this space. Have you thought about taking your business out of your home and opening a dedicated store?"

Only a million times a day, Brandi thought. She dropped her chin to her chest, averting his gaze. The one benefit of public humiliation was her friends and family had witnessed the wedding fiasco and knew her plans to open her store were in a holding pattern. She didn't want to rehash it and look like a loser to Adam, too.

Concern blanketed his features. "What's wrong?"

"Nothing. I'm fine."

"You're not fine," he said. "Why did my asking about opening a store upset you?"

Brandi sighed, still looking at the floor. "Because I'd saved for years and finally found the perfect spot to do just that," she said. "But the money went elsewhere and I had to forget about my big plans."

Adam touched a curved knuckle to her chin and lifted it until her eyes met his. It was completely innocent until their gazes locked, shifting the gesture into something altogether different.

Brandi watched the concern in his eyes morph into longing, and it made her insides quiver in anticipation.

"Perhaps it's time you had a new plan," he said and lowered his lips to hers.

He'd only meant to comfort her.

Then Adam made the mistake of looking into those big, brown eyes, and his noble intentions faltered.

Just one taste, he vowed. A tiny sample to satisfy his curiosity and he'd get back to his reason for being there in the first place.

He closed the scant inch separating them and brushed his lips against hers. God, she tasted good. Even better than he'd imagined. Honey sweet, like a ripe exotic fruit reserved to satiate the palates of kings.

Brandi's lips parted with a breathless sigh, and it was all the invitation he needed.

Adam leaned in and took her mouth, stroking it with his tongue. He groaned as her lush body melted into his.

Everything about this woman was soft except the hard peaks of her breasts against his chest.

Brandi's fingers slid up his forearms to his shoulders. She cradled the back of his neck with her hands and drew him closer.

He responded by deepening the kiss, keeping a tight grip around her waist as well as his control. Adam resisted the urge to let his hands slip beneath her silky shirt and touch skin he knew would feel like satin. He fought the natural instinct to unhook the clasp on her bra and hold the delicious weight of her breasts in his palms.

Adam knew if he allowed his fingertips the pleasure of teasing her already taut nipples or his hands the delight of cupping her sweet bottom, their very first kiss would end with them both naked and tangled in the sheets of the nearest bed.

Brandi broke off the kiss and her arms fell from around his neck. "That was…" she began breathlessly.

Adam dipped his head until it touched her forehead. "What I've wanted to do ever since I saw you in the park."

"Really?"

She sounded surprised, so he confirmed it. "I haven't been able to get you off my mind."

"I don't get it. All those beautiful women in my exercise class. I can't believe you even noticed me."

He pressed the hard evidence of his attraction against her belly, and her breath caught. He watched her teeth sink into her kiss-swollen bottom lip.

"I more than noticed you. I wanted you then, and I want you now," he said, his voice reduced to a husky whisper. "I believe you feel the exact same way."

Brandi took a step backward, and he reluctantly let her go. Already he missed the heat of her body.

"I could deny it, but we'd both know I was lying," she said.

"So what happens now?" Adam asked.

He knew what he wanted to happen. He'd played the scenario in his head all afternoon. The two of them on a flat surface, her thick thighs wrapped around his waist while he buried himself to the hilt. It had been a long time since Adam had wanted a woman as badly as he craved this one.

She stared up at him, the passion in her eyes just scant moments ago replaced with an emotion he couldn't quite place.

"Nothing."

Puzzled, Adam rubbed the back of his neck, still tingling from her touch. He couldn't have heard her right. Not after she'd confessed the attraction he felt toward her was mutual.

"Why not?"

"Because chocolate isn't the only thing I've declared off-limits."

Adam moved toward her, closing the space she'd tried to put between them.

"First my chocolate and now my kisses. Tell me, Brandi, why do you insist on turning down the very things you should be enjoying to the fullest?"

Chapter 5

God help her she did enjoy what this man offered, and she didn't like it one bit.

What was wrong with her?

A week ago, she didn't think it possible for anything or anyone to weaken her resolve to stay clear of chocolate and men. In less than twenty-four hours, Adam had managed to do both.

Apparently, she'd underestimated the potent lure of chocolate and the intoxicating feeling of being kissed by a man she was wildly attracted to.

How long had it been since a simple kiss had left her weak-kneed and practically panting for more? Her ex's certainly hadn't. That's what made the man standing before her all the more dangerous and strictly forbidden.

Brandi walked to her desk on the other side of the room. She pulled a pen from a drawer, and he arched a brow. His expression made it obvious her rifling through the drawer hadn't fooled him. He knew exactly why she'd retreated to the safety of her desk.

Adam crossed the room in three long strides. Leaning forward, he placed his palms flat on the desktop. "Sooooo," he said, drawing out the word. "What exactly do you have against pleasure?"

Oh, he was smooth, Brandi thought, like the velvety ganache center of a to-die-for truffle.

"I'm not against pleasure," she replied firmly. "I just know it often comes with consequences."

"They don't necessarily have to be bad ones."

"Unless they involve chocolate or men, which both have been disastrous for me."

"Why not give both another chance?"

"That's not going to happen."

"Okay, you've already explained your reason for abstaining from chocolate," he said. "But why men? Or more importantly, why avoid being thoroughly kissed by a man who would love nothing more than to kiss you again?" He leaned closer, their bodies separated by her desk, but his tempting lips only a breath away. "And again."

Brandi swallowed hard. "We've barely known each other a day. Why would I confide in you?"

"Because it seems like you could use someone to talk to and sometimes strangers make the best confidants."

"I've never heard that."

He gave a charming smile. "Okay, I made it up, but it makes sense. I'm a neutral party with no stake in the matter."

Brandi's eyes narrowed. "A neutral party who wants to feed me chocolate and get me into bed."

Adam chuckled. "Well, that, too." He came around the desk, reached for her hand and gave it a gentle tug. "Grab your coat. We'll go out and talk over coffee."

He led her out of her office, through the dining room and back to her living room.

"But I already made some," she said, gesturing to the now cold mugs.

"It'll be my treat. Besides, it's the weekend, and there's just something sad about two single people being cooped up inside on a Saturday night, don't you think?"

She cast a glance back to her office. "I still have work to do."

Adam nudged her with his elbow. "Come on," he coaxed. "There's a coffeehouse a few blocks from here I've wanted to try all week, but the name escapes me…."

"You must mean Jolt's. They just opened a month ago. I haven't been there yet, either."

"Good. We can try it together," he said "We'll walk over, and you can show me around the neighborhood."

"I don't know," Brandi hedged.

"No chocolate. No kissing." He raised one hand and splayed the other one over his heart. "I promise we'll only indulge in overpriced caffeinated beverages and good conversation."

Brandi laughed and finally relented. She was just being silly. He'd asked her to share a cup of coffee, not join him for an illicit tryst.

They made a quick stop next door for Adam's jacket before heading out. The sting of crisp night air on her face had been refreshing when they'd initially walked out of their building, but two blocks later Brandi shivered inside of her wool coat.

"Cold?" Adam asked.

"I'm fine." She jammed her hands into her pockets.

Adam pulled his scarf from around his neck and draped it around hers. His body heat clung to the soft cashmere, and Brandi felt the warmth all the way to her toes.

The residential streets leading to the planned community's town center were quiet, except for the sound of their footsteps hitting the sidewalk and the wind whistling through the barren tree limbs. A full moon and the glow illuminating from windows of the apartments and single-family homes lit their path.

"So what happened to the money you'd earmarked to expand your business?" Adam asked, breaking the silence.

"I used it to reimburse my mother for my wedding."

"Wedding? Hold on." He stopped midstep on the sidewalk and exhaled sharply. "You never mentioned being married."

She placed a hand on his biceps. "I'm not," she said. "My ex-fiancé is."

He paused for half a beat. "You lost me somewhere between wedding and ex-fiancé."

With a heavy sigh, Brandi began. "While I waited at the church with two hundred of our closest friends and relatives, the groom married another woman at a chapel in Vegas."

Adam said nothing, but took the hand she'd rested on his biceps and tucked it in the crook of his arm as they resumed walking.

"My non-wedding was embarrassing enough, more for my mother than me," Brandi continued. "I didn't want her to pay the price financially, too. So I drained my savings so she wouldn't be out of pocket."

She left out the part about how she'd mistakenly believed giving her mom the money would put an end to her harangues on how mortifying Brandi's being jilted was for *her.* Instead, it had only stopped Jolene from complaining about how much the debacle had cost.

"So I'd be correct in assuming your moron-of-an-ex's poor judgment is the reason you're on a man sabbatical?"

Brandi nodded. She hated rehashing the story, but it was best Adam knew upfront where she stood and pursuing her was pointless.

"I'm not him," he said firmly.

"It doesn't matter," Brandi replied. "Relationships are a lot of work, and right now I need to put all of my effort into my business."

The finality of her words hung in the air as the dark, quiet residential streets gave way to the bright lights of their community's newly opened town center. Although it was still under construction, a smattering of shops and restaurants had already opened for business. Window signs promised a bookstore, cupcake shop and day spa were coming soon.

Jolt's Coffee, which still had the grand-opening banner draped above the entrance, appeared to have already become a popular neighborhood spot.

Adam held the door open and Brandi walked inside. Strains of soft jazz music, the buzz of conversation and aroma of freshly ground coffee beans surrounded her. In contrast to the shop's logo, a coffee mug split in half by a lightning bolt, the place had a laid-back ambience.

There were the standard table and chairs and a couple of overstuffed chairs arranged in a way to promote conversation. After months of weekends hidden away in her condo, Brandi had to admit it felt good to be stepping out on a Saturday night.

Even if it was just a stroll down the street with a neighbor.

While the majority of the tables were occupied, there wasn't a line at the counter.

Brandi ordered a coffee concoction with nonfat milk, sweetened by a sugar substitute, while Adam opted for black coffee.

They settled on a high bistro table in front of the window with a view of the street. Brandi stared out at the people going in and out of the various stores and eateries.

If the shops in her working-class neighborhood drew a steady stream of customers, she could only imagine the store traffic in the trendier area she had wanted to locate her handbag boutique. Arm Candy would do a brisk business there.

"Have you applied for a small-business loan?" Adam asked without preamble.

Brandi felt an unexpected twinge of disappointment at his question. Apparently, she'd done a good job of getting through to him, and he'd dropped the idea of them being more than neighbors. It's what she wanted, right? To stay focused on her business.

"The bank turned me down." She shrugged. "Good credit, but no collateral and no savings."

He asked her about her profit margin, and his eyes widened at how much her bottom line had increased over the few years she'd been in business.

"I'm surprised they didn't grant it. From the little I've seen and heard, your business seems like a good risk," he said.

"The loan officer said a few years ago an application like mine would have been easily approved, but the current economic climate has tightened restrictions and made them less apt to take a chance on new ventures."

"And I'm guessing borrowing from your family…"

"Is out of the question," Brandi finished. She sampled her coffee, which could have used a few teaspoons of real sugar and a dollop of whipped cream. "Like I told you earlier, my younger sister is getting married next month."

"So what's your business plan?"

"I've started saving again, but it'll take time to get my bank balance up to where it was before."

Adam folded his arms across the table and leaned forward. "What if I told you there were other ways for you to get money?" He raised a brow and a grin spread over his face. "And that I have a proposition for you."

"I'd say I'm two seconds from dumping hot coffee in your lap."

Adam glanced from the curl of steam rising from Brandi's coffee to the offended look on her face.

"Whoa." He held up his hands as understanding dawned. "You've got it all wrong."

It had been a poor choice of words on his part, but an idea had come to him that might solve both of their problems. Now all he had to do was sell his scowling neighbor on it.

Adam took the precautionary measure of pushing the drinks aside before launching into his pitch. "I'm talking about alternative and *completely legitimate* sources for seed money."

"Well, don't keep me in suspense." She didn't look mad enough to throw coffee, but her expression remained guarded.

"The company I used to work for—as well as a lot of other major corporations and foundations—have programs that make loans to fledgling entrepreneurs like yourself."

"Really?" She leaned forward in her seat.

"There's nontraditional financing help out there like microfinancing, crowdfunding and peer-to-peer lending," he said. "With them, potential and your business plan are taken into consideration, not just collateral and credit scores."

"I don't know," Brandi said. "Sounds too good to be true."

Adam pulled out his smart phone and pulled up the web browser. Moments later he showed her an article about a woman who'd taken her cupcake business from a street cart to a space in a mall food court thanks to microloans from two large corporations.

"Wow. I'd never heard of this kind of help. I thought it was the bank or nothing," she said after reading it. Brandi handed him back his phone and slid their coffee back in front of them. "Thank you." A hint of a smile returned to her face. "I'm going to look into it as soon as I get home."

"Keep in mind, you also have a valuable resource with over ten years of executive experience living right next door to you." Adam eyed her over the rim of his coffee mug. "I could point out the best opportunities and weed out the bad ones with high interest rates and hidden fees."

She took a sip of coffee and appeared to be absorbing what he'd said.

"I'd also help you make your application absolutely irresistible," he said. "Of course, I can't guarantee you funding, but I know what I'd look for in a candidate looking for funding."

"And you'd do this for a woman you've known for all of twenty-four hours, because?"

"I need your help, too," he said. "The suggestions for my cake were right on target. It took you two seconds to figure out the perfect tweak to a recipe I'd been working on for days."

"But I'm no expert. I just love chocolate," she excused.

"That's enough for me. I just want you to taste what I have and tell me what you think."

"Ordinarily, I'd jump at the chance, but..."

He nodded. "Your sister's wedding."

"I ordered my maid-of-honor dress earlier today. It's already a tight fit, and if I help you I won't fit into it at all."

He nodded. "I understand how important this wedding is to you, but so is getting your business out of your spare bedroom," he said. "You don't have to make a decision tonight. All I ask is you take a few days to think it over."

She nodded. "Okay, but I won't change my mind."

Chapter 6

It had taken two cups of black coffee to give Brandi the kick in the pants she needed to face Monday and her morning classes.

Although she hadn't seen Adam since they'd returned from the coffee shop Saturday night, his presence lingered throughout Sunday with the aroma of chocolate continuing to seep into her place. Even worse, every movement she heard through their shared wall caused her to wonder what he was doing and to replay their kiss in her head.

Teenaged-girl giggles erupted from the back of her freshman drawing class, and Brandi corralled her wandering thoughts. Adam had commandeered her mind all weekend, and it was past time for her common sense to take back control.

She continued walking slowly around the room observing the emerging drawings on her students' sketchpads. This morning they were starting a weeklong lesson on lines and shading, using kitchen utensils from home as models.

Brandi paused at the desk of a lanky freshman attempting to draw a slotted spoon. "Light pressure with your pencil, Brandon. Instead of pressing harder to make it darker, use light strokes and go over the area several times."

The boy grunted his acknowledgment of her suggestion and yawned.

It was a week into the new year, but the kids she taught at Central High School were still recovering from the Christmas holidays and readjusting to the school routine. Students in her earlier classes had been just as lethargic.

"This looks like crap."

Brandi looked up as Ashley Lowell flung her pencil, and she weaved through desks toward the teen attempting to sketch a balloon whisk.

"What's going on?" Brandi surveyed the page in Ashley's sketchpad, which featured more eraser marks than ones made with graphite pencil.

"I keep messing up." Frustration laced Ashley's tone.

Brandi knew the problem. The perfectionism the teen brought to her other classes didn't serve her well in art. The honor roll student had to learn how to lighten up. Mistakes were part of the process.

"Try it again, but this time no erasing," Brandi said.

Ashley drew the lines again. "See what I mean." The teen reached for the eraser, but Brandi quickly covered it with her hand.

The bell chimed signaling the end of the period, and the familiar bustle of students gathering their things to move on to their next class or lunch ensued.

"We'll pick this up again tomorrow, Ashley," Brandi said. "Meanwhile, try to remember that you can't draw it right until you've drawn it wrong."

When the last student filed out the class, Brandi stifled another yawn. Tonight, she was going to get a good night's sleep—even if she had to check into a hotel to do it.

"Ready to go nuke lunch?"

Brandi saw her friend and fellow teacher, Lynn Myers, standing in the open classroom doorway. She started to smile, and then caught the look on the computer science teacher's face.

"What's wrong?" Brandi asked.

"I guess you haven't b ..n to your box today."

Brandi shook her head. "Not yet. What's going on?"

"We all got letters from the superintendent of schools. Ten percent of Central's staff is going to be laid off at the end of the school year," Lynn said as they made their way down the hallway. They'd done lunchroom duty last week, so this week they were free to eat in the teachers' lounge.

Brandi heaved a sigh. It wasn't as if they hadn't been expecting it. Only back when the school board's budget was initially slashed, Brandi had expected to be a married woman running her own boutique. "I'd better start working on my résumé."

"We might be safe," Lynn said. "After all, we're both past the ten-year mark here."

Brandi shrugged. They'd both started teaching at Central fresh out of college. Lynn, who was savvy in various areas of computer science and web design, could find a job elsewhere if necessary. "You'll be fine, but I doubt my seniority will matter. I teach art, which isn't considered essential." She retrieved her frozen diet meal from the community fridge, peeled back the plastic and stuck it in the microwave. "I'll be one of the first to go."

"Maybe not." Lynn sounded more hopeful than reassuring.

Brandi pulled her nuked lunch from the microwave after

the chime and Lynn took her turn. A second chime later, they were both seated at a table with their meals and diet sodas.

"I've got Asian Delight," Brandi said, "but I'm up for a trade if you're willing."

"Sure. It doesn't matter to me. After a while, all of these low-cal meals taste like hot slop."

Lynn had started her diet before the holidays, and Brandi could already see evidence of weight loss. Her friend's round face was more angular, and her stomach was noticeably flatter.

"It'll be worth it when you're romping on a Hawaiian beach in a string bikini," Brandi said.

Last year, Lynn had married her second husband, James, and when school let out for spring break she and her hunky, new firefighter hubby planned to go to Hawaii for their long-awaited honeymoon.

"At this point, I'm ready to trade that stupid bikini in for a cheeseburger and fries."

Brandi took a bite of her swapped ravioli. "You're right, this is hot slop."

"So how did the dress shopping go?" Lynn poked around the Asian Delight with a plastic fork. "Your mother didn't drive you to drink, did she?"

"Almost, but we did find a dress." Brandi recapped how she'd sized down, while her mother had purchased the same dress for her two sizes larger.

"Sheesh, I know she's your mom and all, but I don't know how you put up with her," Lynn said.

"Sometimes I don't, either." Brandi shrugged.

Inwardly, she knew the reasons. Before he died, her father had made her promise to look after her mother and sister. Secondly, her mother hadn't always been so harsh.

Brandi used to be the envy of the other kids for having the sweetest mother on their block.

Deep down, Brandi waited for that softer side of Jolene to resurface.

"You're not going to give her the satisfaction of needing that bigger dress, are you?" Lynn asked.

"There's no way I'm falling off the diet wagon," Brandi said, then added, *"again."*

"Again?" Lynn raised a brow. "You pawned off your chocolate stash on your students. Don't tell me you went out and bought more."

Brandi shook her head. "Would you believe I was accosted and force-fed chocolate?"

Her friend threw her head back and laughed. "First, it was imaginary smells. Now you're the victim of chocolate bullies? It's only been a week, and this diet is already getting to you."

Brandi popped the top on her can of diet soda and took a sip. "Turns out those smells were real, and my new neighbor is responsible for them as well as my temporary lapse."

"Neighbor? I thought the condo next to yours was vacant."

"Not anymore. It's now the home of a guy prepping for, get this," Brandi said, "the International Chocolate Pastry Competition."

"You have got to be kidding me," Lynn said.

"If it's a joke, it's on me. I went over there to ask him to stop and ended up walking into a chocolate croissant and tart-filled landmine. One minute, I'm complaining about the smell, and the next I'm sampling the best chocolate hazelnut torte I've ever tasted."

"Ooh, so what does he look like?"

Brandi stared down at her lunch as images of the dark-chocolate-dipped hunk and the kiss they'd shared played through her mind.

"He's okay." She speared a piece of ravioli with her plastic fork and stuck it in her mouth. She chewed and swallowed quickly before her taste buds could revolt.

"Just okay, huh?"

"All right, he's drop-dead gorgeous." Brandi blew out a breath. Her friend would draw it out of her eventually, so she might as well spill it. "And my diet wasn't the only pledge I broke."

Lynn dropped her fork and stared, mouth open.

"Did you two…?" She waggled her brows, while sticking the index finger of one hand into the rolled fist of the other.

Brandi giggled and smacked at her friend's hands. "God, you're as bad as the kids," she said. "We only kissed."

Her friend's face broke out in a huge grin. "Well, it's about time."

"Actually, there's more. He made me an offer I hadn't planned on considering, but now I'm tempted to take him up on it."

Lynn abandoned the pretense of trying to eat her lunch. She leaned forward in her chair, and Brandi filled her in on her last encounter with Adam.

"So are you going to do it?"

Brandi shook her head. "I don't know. There's no way I can eat chocolate and fit into my dress for Erin's wedding."

"Tough call," Lynn said. "I know you want to show Wesley what he missed and shut your mom up, but you're going to have to figure out if it's worth passing up a chance to take Arm Candy to the next level."

After her last class, Brandi ventured to her inbox in the school's administration office where her copy of the letter awaited. Her eyes skimmed over the words. While it didn't say so specifically, she knew her days of teaching at Central High were numbered.

She crammed the missive back into the envelope and stuck it in her tote. Still, worries of her financial future plagued her as she steered her car toward home.

Brandi had abandoned the habit of driving past the Green Hills storefront where she'd hoped to locate her store after it had been rented out. What was the point? The prime spot was now a children's clothing store.

But after today's letter she couldn't help turning onto the familiar street for a peek at what could have been. What *should* have been.

"Oh, my God," she whispered.

The bright red-and-white sign on the window caught her eye first, the words *FOR LEASE*. She braked abruptly, earning a horn honk from the car behind her. She pulled her car over to the curb and grabbed a pen from the glove compartment, her hand trembling as she scribbled down the leasing agent's phone number.

Brandi couldn't help envisioning the storefront windows of the terra-cotta brick building shaded by crisp black awnings adorned with the Arm Candy logo in white. Her brain fast-forwarded to showcasing her handbags in those very same windows.

All of a sudden, her decision about Adam's offer didn't seem complicated at all.

Adam whisked eggs, sugar and vanilla into the melted chocolate mixture and poured the filling into a warm walnut crust. His phone rang just as he slid the tart pan into the oven.

Frowning at the distraction, he snatched the phone off the counter intending to shut it off. He saw his grandmother's photo flash across the small screen and any irritation vanished.

"Bonsoir, Mémé," he said, taking the seven-hour time difference between Nashville and Paris into account.

The two touched based with each other by email daily, especially since Adam had given the widowed octogenarian a tablet computer for Christmas. So when they spoke on the phone or via Skype they got right to the point, not wasting time with small talk.

Immediately, his *grand-mère* inquired about his preparations for the competition.

"Ah, *comme ci comme ça,*" he replied. So far, his day in the kitchen had been hit and miss. He'd nearly perfected his take on chocolate soufflé cake. However, his dark chocolate mille-feuille, layers of puff pastry and filling widely referred to as a Napoleon, hadn't come close to his grandfather's rendition.

"Your grandfather would be proud of you," Catherine Rousseau said softly in French, as if she'd known what he was thinking. "And he'll be smiling down on you from heaven when there's once again a chocolate pastry champion in our family."

"I'll do my best, but it's just the amateur division. It's not like Grandpa winning the master pastry chef prize," Adam said.

"You underestimate yourself and all you learned from him," she said. "I still remember how you used to trail him around the bakery when you visited."

His grandparents had lived above the bakery they owned, and Adam could still remember being awakened every morning by the sweet scents of sugar and butter.

Adam told her he had a *tarte au chocolat* in the oven, and then set the timer so he wouldn't get caught up in conversation and forget it. His grandmother was updating him on the dinner party she'd attended earlier that evening, when he heard a knock at his door.

He smiled at the sight of Brandi and beckoned her inside. She wore her green wool coat and a tartan-plaid tote was slung over her shoulder. He felt the outdoor chill emanating from her and figured she must have come straight from work without stopping off at her place first.

Adam continued to talk to his grandmother, while Brandi dropped her tote on the kitchen island and seated herself on one of the chairs facing it. Not that there was much choice of seating. He really was going to have to do something about his lack of furniture.

"Ah Mémé, vous êtes une belle femme," Adam told his grandmother, after she mentioned a gentleman in his seventies who'd flirted shamelessly with her throughout the party.

"Get out of here," Catherine replied in English laced with a Southern lilt that gave away her American roots.

A few minutes later, his grandmother, who he'd already heard yawn twice, bid him good-night.

"Bonne nuit, Mémé."

Adam switched off the mobile and placed it in a kitchen drawer. He wanted to give his visitor his full attention. "This is a pleasant surprise," he said.

Brandi had shed her coat, and his eyes traveled from her formfitting pencil skirt down to shapely legs encased in black tights and crossed at the knee. He imagined those legs wrapped around his waist and felt his groin tighten.

"You speak French?" Brandi asked.

Adam reluctantly tore his gaze from her legs. He held up his thumb and forefinger leaving an inch separating the digits. *"Un peu, et vous?"*

"If you're asking if I do, then the answer is no. I took a year of it in high school, but don't remember much," she said. "But you sounded as if you know more than just a little."

"That was my grandmother on the phone. She lives in Paris, and I picked up a bit of the language as a kid when I visited her and my grandfather over school breaks," he said.

"Your grandparents are French?" Brandi asked.

"Actually, my mother's father was a Frenchman. Her mother was born and raised right here in Nashville. While on a semester abroad from Fisk, she met and married my grandfather," he said. "She's lived in Paris for over sixty years now, so she tends to forget English is her first language."

"How romantic." Brandi sighed dreamily. "I've always wanted to visit Paris. Is it really as beautiful as everyone says?"

"I'm probably biased because I have so many wonderful memories of being there with my grandparents, but it truly is the most magnificent city in the world."

"And are your parents here?"

"They were, but they're both dead now. My mother passed when I was young, and my father died of a massive coronary a few months ago."

"I'm sorry for your loss."

He nodded his head in acknowledgment. "What about you? Your parents live nearby?"

"My mother does. My dad died when I was in high school."

"Any siblings besides your engaged sister?"

"No, that's it. What about you?"

"A younger brother."

"Is he who you were playing basketball with in the park?"

Adam laughed. "I was trying to play. Thanks to you, he beat the pants off me."

"Me? What did I do?"

"You distracted me." He caught her gaze and held it. "I couldn't stop gawking at you."

The oven timer sounded, and Adam pulled the tart from the oven. It smelled good, and if he thought so after smelling chocolate all day long, he hoped it had the desired effect on his pretty neighbor.

"So have you thought any more about what we discussed Saturday night?" He placed the tart on the wire rack to cool.

"Yes, in fact that's why I'm here. I've decided to take you up on your offer to help me secure alternative financing for my business."

Relief washed over him. Deep down he knew it wasn't solely because he needed her, he was also grateful for an excuse to spend time with her. "I'm delighted," he said. "However, you do remember there were strings attached."

Brandi nodded. "I haven't forgotten the terms."

"So what changed your mind? Last time we talked you'd all but turned me down."

Brandi heaved a sigh. "Two reasons. First, it appears school budget cuts are going to cut me right out of a job at the end of the term. Secondly, the space I wanted to lease for my boutique is suddenly available again," she said. "I'm taking both things as a sign it's time for me to move Arm Candy forward sooner rather than later."

"Then we have a deal." Adam extended his hand.

She paused a moment before taking it, but her hesitance merely delayed the inevitable sizzle of electricity that spiked every time they touched. Adam looked down at their joined hands and back at her. He knew she felt it, too. And like him, she was probably thinking of the kiss they'd shared the other day.

A kiss he hadn't been able to get off his mind.

He leaned over the counter and touched his lips to hers. Damn. If only he could develop a recipe that mimicked the full-bodied sweetness of her mouth, it would be the hands-down winner of any competition.

Brandi broke off the all-too-brief kiss, but not the sexual tension that lingered in its wake. She leaned back in the chair and folded her arms across her chest. "I've agreed to your terms, now it's time you heard mine."

He rounded the counter and sat on the seat next to her. "I'm listening."

"Things between us have to remain strictly business. That means no more kissing and certainly nothing beyond," she said.

"If that's what you want."

Brandi nodded. "It is."

"Then I'll abide by your wishes."

Adam would just have to keep his attraction to her in check, because as badly as he wanted to taste her mouth again—he needed her tasting chocolate more.

Chapter 7

The evening after agreeing to Adam's proposal, Brandi was having second thoughts.

About their deal and her attire.

She stared in the mirror at the second outfit she'd changed into to meet with him tonight. Dark bootcut jeans hugged her hips and a red sweater with a deep V-neck showed off her cleavage. Ruby earrings dangled from her earlobes while her hair, salon fresh from a standing weekly appointment, had the kind of glossy curls only a stylist could achieve.

A slick of red gloss and a spritz of her favorite perfume added the perfect finishing touches. She looked good.

Too good.

Brandi frowned at her reflection. She'd made hot date effort, when she should be doing everything in her power to put a damper on the fireworks that sparked every time she and Adam exchanged glances.

She kicked off her strappy red heels, and yanked the sweater over her head. Tossing the sweater on the bed, Brandi went to her closet and rifled through the racks of clothing.

She unearthed a faded pink velour track suit, a decade-old throwback from J. Lo's first fashion collection, and a T-shirt that had seen better days.

Moments later, she surveyed her revamped appearance in the mirror. Age had stretched the pants and hoodie enough so they fit her bigger body. She tissued off the lip gloss and swept her hair up into a haphazard ponytail.

"That's better," Brandi told the shabbily dressed woman staring back at her in the mirror. "If Adam has any illusions about being attracted to me—this ought to shatter them."

She laughed to herself and grabbed her laptop to take over to his place.

Chocolate, the scent even stronger than in her condo, hit her hard as she stood in front of Adam's door. She'd had an extra-light lunch and skipped dinner in preparation of the delights awaiting her. Her stomach rumbled in anticipation.

The door swung open before she could knock and an angry face blazed down at hers.

"Um…I was looking for Adam," a startled Brandi told the vaguely familiar man. "Is he here?"

Adam appeared in the doorway behind his obviously annoyed visitor, and she was relieved when a smile lit his handsome features at the sight of her. Still, his disposition didn't appear any sunnier than the other man's.

"If this is a bad time, I can come back later," she said.

"Not at all." Adam inclined his head toward the other man. "Brandi Collins, meet my brother, Kyle Ellison. Kyle, my neighbor, Brandi. Kyle was just leaving."

Kyle gave her the once-over with one sweep of his eyes and something in them dismissed her.

"Nice to meet you," Brandi said, regretting her dressed-down appearance. She'd only expected to see Adam tonight.

His brother wore an exquisitely cut, charcoal-gray business suit and a burgundy silk tie. An overcoat was draped over his arm, and the leather gloves in his hand probably cost more than a full month of her schoolteacher paychecks.

"Likewise," Kyle said. He gave her a tight, polite smile, before turning back to Adam. "Since there's no reasoning with you, I'll leave you to your cakes and your company."

Brandi wasn't sure what she'd just witnessed, but the sadness in Adam's eyes as his brother walked away made her heart go out to him.

She reached out and touched a hand to his arm. "It's okay. We can do this another time."

"That's not necessary." He smiled and took her lightly by the elbow to lead her inside. "Sorry you walked into that. Like I told you, my decision to pursue this competition hasn't been very popular."

Brandi had dealt with discouragement from her family, but not on this level. Then again, she'd always played it safe and tried to please everyone. She'd never taken a big leap of faith in herself and her skills like Adam had. Even now, as precarious as it was, she had her teaching job as backup.

He had nothing.

"Have a seat," Adam said.

Brandi looked up and was surprised to see a dining room suite occupied the open area off the kitchen that was completely empty yesterday afternoon.

"Ah, I see your furniture's here," she said, taking in the

contemporary marble table surrounded by six suede chairs. He'd apparently eschewed the traditional china cabinet in lieu of two large bookcases.

"Actually, I bought it this morning, and the furniture store offered same-day delivery," he said. "I can't have us working at the kitchen island."

"You didn't have to go through all this trouble for me." She chewed at her bottom lip. "Especially with you not working right now."

"Don't worry about me. I have savings."

Of course he did, Brandi thought. Once upon a time she did, too.

He pulled out a chair at the table, and Brandi sat down, wondering what he had in store for her. Maybe she'd get to sample yesterday's chocolate tart, which had smelled so good it nearly brought tears to her eyes.

Heather was going to make her pay the price, so she might as well make it worth her while.

"Well, what do you want me to taste first?"

He seated himself in a chair directly across from hers. "Actually, nothing. I thought we'd put you first and focus on your business tonight."

"Oh," Brandi said. The disappointment she felt at not walking into a chocolate smorgasbord was overwhelmed by his statement about putting her first. She couldn't even remember the last time someone had put her concerns over their own.

"Have you eaten?" he asked.

She shook her head. "I wanted to conserve my calories so tonight's splurge wouldn't do as much damage."

"Then have dinner with me."

His offer was as tempting as the aroma of chocolate permeating the room, but it wasn't a good idea.

"I thought we agreed to keep this strictly business."

"We did." Adam's gaze slid downward from her face to the faded hoodie and rumpled T-shirt before once again meeting hers. "And by the way, nice try."

"I don't understand."

"That getup you're wearing," he said. "Sweetheart, it's going to take more than beat-up sweats and a messy hairdo to make me forget I want you."

Brandi gulped audibly. She hadn't expected to be figured out so easily or the clenching of everything in her that was female at the words: *I want you.*

Adam chuckled softly. "Besides, I'm not asking you on a date," he said. "It's simply a business dinner. You know, two people talking business over food. In my old life, I did it all the time."

"Okay, then," Brandi said, feeling foolish at having overreacted.

He rose from the table and crossed the open space into the kitchen. "Good. I'll have it on the table in a few minutes. Hope you like carrot ginger soup."

Brandi nodded. "It's my favorite. I pick up a cup every time I go to Healthy Market."

"Then you'll love this, because that's exactly what I did. I bake, but my cooking skills are limited to the microwave and takeout."

"Good, then you're not perfect. If you cooked, too, I'd have to wonder why you were still single," she said. The words tumbled out of her mouth ahead of her brain.

He gave her a pointed look. "Maybe I've been saving myself for the right woman."

Brandi averted her eyes to avoid the intensity of his stare and abruptly changed the subject. "What can I do to help?"

He shook his head. "I've got it under control."

"At least let me set the table." She abandoned the large table for the kitchen.

Adam nodded and directed her to the cabinets and drawers where he stored dishes and cutlery. They moved through the kitchen and dining areas in comfortable silence, before sitting down to a quick meal of soup, salad and crusty sourdough bread.

No, it wasn't the orgasmic chocolate experience she'd been looking forward to all day, but it was nice sharing an evening meal with someone. In the months after her breakup with Wesley, her dinners had consisted of whatever she picked up at the gourmet candy store or bakery on the way home from work with only the television for company.

"So what got you into handbag design?" Adam asked.

"It's a long story," she said. "Are you sure you want to hear it?"

"Two things you should know about me. One is I don't say things I don't mean, and secondly, I don't waste my time," he said. "So when I say I'd like to hear it, I mean it."

His stark honesty and directness were a relief to Brandi, who was used to her mother's version, which came off as overly critical.

"Well in that case, it started back in high school," Brandi began. "I saw a pretty floral bag in a teen magazine. It was all the rage, and all my friends had one."

She told him how her parents thought the trendy fabric bag was overpriced and refused to buy it. She'd whined to her folks for days about how not having the "it" bag was ruining her social life.

Then one day, her grandmother had overheard.

"Grandma told me to quit whining or she'd give me something to whine about." Brandi laughed at the memory and looked up to see a twinkle of amusement in Adam's eyes.

"She looked over the magazine and declared we could make a bag on her old Singer sewing machine just as good—if not better than that one."

"And did you?" Adam asked and from the curve of a smile on his full lips, Brandi knew he already knew the answer.

She nodded proudly. "Not only that, soon I was making them for all my friends. It wasn't long afterward I began to design and sell my own bags," she said. "Any free time I had after school or on weekends was spent on working on new designs with Grandma."

"So why didn't you pursue it, instead of teaching?"

Brandi sighed. "I'd planned to. I'd even gotten accepted into the Fashion Institute of Technology in New York as an accessories design major." She couldn't help the wistful note in her voice as she remembered.

"You didn't go?" Adam asked.

Brandi shook her head. "My mother was dead set against it. She said it was a pipe dream and insisted I get, what she called, a solid degree in a stable profession. So that's how I ended up teaching high school."

"Didn't your grandmother or maybe your father try to intervene with your mom?"

"I'd like to think they would have, especially my grandmother," she said. "But she and my father were hit by a drunk driver two months before I graduated high school. My grandmother was killed instantly, and Dad died a week later at the hospital."

He reached across the table and covered her hand with his. "You'd told me your father had passed, but I had no idea you lost your grandmother at the same time," he said. "What a tragedy."

Brandi nodded. "Because of how they died, I've never touched alcohol," she said. "I know there are people who drink it responsibly every day, but I could never enjoy it after the devastation it caused my family."

It had been the darkest period of her life, but she was grateful she at least got an opportunity to say goodbye to her father before he died.

He gave her hand a gentle squeeze. "Again, I'm sorry for your loss. My grandmother is my biggest champion."

"So she's not in the contingent of friends and family bothered by your abrupt career change?"

"No, just the opposite," Adam said. "Like the relationship you shared with your grandmother, she and I have always been close. She only wants me to be happy."

"You're lucky to have her," Brandi said.

"Are you and your mother close?"

Brandi shrugged. "We used to be, but that was a long time ago," she said. "Everything changed after my father died."

"Then I feel sorry for her," Adam said. "From the little I know about you, I think she has a very special daughter."

Standing, he released her hand, and she immediately missed the warmth and comfort. Brandi had walked through his door expecting to be overwhelmed by chocolate only to discover the real treat.

Adam Ellison had a good heart. Brandi sighed inwardly as she watched him walk toward the kitchen. If she wasn't careful she might find herself doing something stupider than lusting after him—actually liking him.

Now Adam knew how Brandi felt.

The scent of her perfume wreaked havoc on his senses as they sat side by side at the table.

He leaned in for a closer look of the business plan on

her laptop. Each time he attempted to review the cash-flow statement and break-even analysis, he made the mistake of inhaling and his eyes drifted to the pulse point on the side of her neck.

Adam ached to press his lips to the spot and indulge his senses in the bewitching blend of orange blossoms, gardenias and something uniquely her that stirred a primitive side of his nature he hadn't known existed. At this moment, he wanted nothing more than to strip that ugly outfit off her sexy body, toss her over his shoulder and carry her caveman-style to his bed.

His groin tightened at the thought of touching and kissing every inch of her, and he was grateful the new dining table camouflaged the fact business was the last thing on his mind.

He blinked to clear the sensual fog from his brain and turned his attention back to the numbers on the screen.

Focus.

"You're awfully quiet," Brandi said. "Is it that bad?"

Adam cleared his throat and shifted in his seat. "No. Not at all," he said. "In fact, it's quite impressive."

"Even with the start-up expenses and rent, I believe I can break even within six months and begin turning a profit within a year."

Adam opened the folder filled with the research he'd done before she'd arrived. "I compiled a list of potential microloan sources, which I believe are a better option for you than crowdfunding or peer-to-peer lending. The ones I selected are from reputable sources interested in helping small businesses, and they all have low interest rates and reasonable payback terms. I weeded out the ones looking to capitalize on desperation and the economic downturn with hidden service fees and charges," he said.

Brandi flipped through the stack of papers he handed her.

"I also took the liberty of printing out the online brochures and applications for you," he added.

"Thank you," she said.

Adam opened a second folder. "I kept this one separate because it was particularly interesting," he said. "It's the non-profit foundation arm of a design house targeted at helping women entrepreneurs with fashion-related businesses."

Her eyes lit up, and he brushed off an unexpected wave of satisfaction.

"The designer is offering personal mentoring for one business she feels has the most potential," he said.

"Oh, my God," Brandi exclaimed. "This is Lina Todd. She's huge."

"Is she, now?" Adam asked.

"Of course. She designs everything from dresses to housewares. There's even talk of her doing a collaboration with Target," Brandi said, before pausing to take a breath. "Wait a minute, she also has a men's line. You must have heard of her."

"There may be a tie or two with her name on it in my closet," Adam said, knowing full well a visit to the designer's men's boutique the last time he was in New York City had left his black American Express card smoking.

Brandi's brown eyes narrowed, and he burst into laughter under their scrutiny.

"Stop teasing," she said. "You know Lina Todd is the name at the top of fashion's 'it' list."

"Okay, okay." Adam held his hands up in mock defense. "I've heard of her. More importantly, I think this could be the perfect opportunity for you, but you'll have to act fast."

He directed her to the last page of the application, where he'd already circled the deadline in red.

"But that's the day after tomorrow. I have a full-time

job. There's no way I could possibly pull everything they want together by then," she said. "And it says if you're interested in being the business selected for personal mentoring sessions from Lina, they suggest you send in a video."

Adam watched the enthusiasm drain from her face, and his gut twisted.

"I guess I'd better look at the other ones," she said, putting the application for the microloan from the Lina Todd Foundation aside.

Adam stared at the discarded application. He'd been so focused on the loan terms he'd missed the part about the video.

He thought about all the work he had to do. The date of the chocolate competition would be here before he knew it, and while thanks to Brandi he had his first entry, he was still no closer to making a final decision on the second.

Adam picked up the Lina Todd application. Brandi was right. There wasn't enough time, he thought, and then he caught the disappointed look in her eyes.

"Let's go for it." The words came out before his brain could stop them.

"But how?"

"We can focus on the written part of the application and supporting documents tonight. Tomorrow when you get off work we'll shoot the video."

"But I don't have a video camera."

"I do." Fortunately for her, he'd recently purchased a camera to shoot photos of his culinary creations. It also took high-definition video.

"But I have no idea what to say or do for the video," Brandi hedged.

"No more 'buts,'" Adam said firmly. "You have tonight and all day tomorrow to figure that out."

A smile tugged at the corner of her mouth. "Do you really think we can pull it off?"

Adam mentally noted her use of the word *we* and discovered he liked being on this woman's side. He'd started out only helping her so she could get busy taste-testing his recipes.

Now he was genuinely rooting for her to be successful.

Adam opened a new browser window on her laptop and pulled up Overnight Express's website. "We have until midnight tomorrow. That's the cutoff for the last delivery to New York City," he said. "And yes, I think we can do it."

"I can't believe it." Her voice quivered with excitement. "Up until now I thought it would be years before I could get Arm Candy out of my spare room and into its own boutique. Now I actually have a chance at getting funding and advice from Lina Todd."

She held up her hand, as if to calm herself. "I understand it's a long shot at best, but just a sliver of a chance to get business input from her is the opportunity of a lifetime."

Her elation was infectious, and it was hard for Adam not to get caught up in the swell of it. Already a beautiful woman, the big smile on her face elevated her to stunning. He swallowed hard, resisting the urge to caress her smooth brown cheek and get lost in those big, brown eyes.

Adam didn't pretend to like or understand the limitations she'd put on their relationship, but he wouldn't violate them.

She would.

And he'd bide his time until his neighbor realized the underlying current of sexual tension buzzing between them wouldn't be denied.

Brandi's voice broke into his thoughts. Adam started to

ask her to repeat what she'd said, when she threw her arms around him and planted a kiss on his mouth.

Stunned, Adam didn't have time to respond or even savor the brief connection before she abruptly pulled back. She raised her fingertips to her lips.

"I didn't mean... I mean... Sorry, I guess I got overly excited," she stammered. "It won't happen again."

Adam simply nodded. Not because he agreed with her, but because it would happen again, and next time her excitement would be of an entirely different nature.

Chapter 8

Brandi sprinted through the school parking lot toward her car.

The principal had called a mandatory meeting after school to discuss the letters they'd all received yesterday. The extra hour and a half tacked on to their day hadn't told Central High's staff anything they didn't already know. Soon, some of them would be out of a job.

Brandi unearthed her cell phone from her purse and texted Adam she was on her way. She'd sent him one earlier when she'd first found out about the meeting, saying she'd be delayed.

Adam.

For the hundredth time today she touched her fingertips to her lips, which still tingled at the memory of the brief contact with his. The kiss itself had been innocent, but not the yearning for more that followed her out of his condo and into her dreams.

She snatched her hand away from her mouth and yanked open her car door.

"Quit making a big deal out of nothing," she mumbled.

Adam had understood it had only been a quick peck in the heat of the moment. Unlike her, he hadn't let his imagination turn it into a sizzling lovemaking session with her straddling him atop that new dining room table of his.

"Don't even go there," she said.

The last thing she needed was to muck up her head lusting after her neighbor, especially now, when it finally seemed like she was making inroads toward expanding Arm Candy.

Brandi threw the car's gear into Reverse and backed out of her designated parking space. She winced as her tires squealed against the pavement and hoped her students hadn't spotted her burning rubber escaping the school parking lot.

Her cell phone rang, and Brandi plucked it off the passenger's seat. She glanced at the small screen and briefly debated whether to let it go to voice mail. In the end, her conscience wouldn't allow it.

"Hi, Mom."

"Where are you?" Jolene Collins sounded ticked off, which didn't bode well for pleasant conversation.

"In my car. There was a meeting after scho—"

"Good," her mother interrupted, "then you're on your way here. I was expecting you over an hour ago."

Damn. She was supposed to go by her mom's to take care of a to-do list of minor maintenance things her mother needing doing around her house. She'd picked up the supplies she needed at the big-box hardware store a few days ago, so they were already in the trunk of her car. However, in the excitement of working with Adam on her business, it had slipped her mind she was due over there today.

"I'm sorry, Mom. I forgot," she said. "Can I come by tomorrow instead?"

Silence.

"Mom? You still there?"

Another beat of silence followed by a long-suffering sigh.

"Of course I'm here," she said. "Where else would I be? After all, my daughter said she'd be here today."

"Something important has come up, but I promise to stop by tomorrow right after work."

"And what's more important than you giving your poor, widowed mother a hand?"

Brandi groaned inwardly. A huge part of her wished she could tell her mother what she and Adam were doing, but she didn't need the discouragement that was sure to come. She'd wait until she secured a microloan, hopefully the one from Lina Todd, before telling her mom she'd revived her plan to open a boutique.

"Mom, I'll help you tomorrow. I'll even bring takeout from your favorite Chinese restaurant for dinner, okay?"

It wasn't as if her mom had to rearrange anything more important than a spa appointment or bridge game with her girlfriends.

Last year, after her husband's unexpected death, Brandi's mother sold the successful temping agency for administrative office workers she'd started for a tidy sum. The windfall, combined with the generous provisions from Brandi's father, had left Jolene Collins very well-off.

"Don't bother. I'll just dig the ladder out of the garage and change that blown bulb on the ceiling light fixture myself," her mother said. "Hopefully, I won't fall and break a hip."

Brandi checked her side-view mirror and merged her car into interstate traffic headed in the direction of her condo.

"Mom, please. Just leave everything until tomorrow," she repeated. "Besides, that light needs a special bulb. I've already picked it up."

Her mother treated her to another sigh, this one even more drawn out than the first. "It's times like this when I miss your father the most. He never let me down."

Like a puppeteer controlling a marionette, her mother always knew which strings to pull. Nothing, except the mention of her father, would have detoured Brandi from her beeline to Adam's place.

Her father's last words to her echoed in her head as Brandi took the next exit off the interstate and reversed her direction.

"I need to know you'll look after your mother for me and your sister," he'd rasped from his hospital bed.

Brandi was determined to keep her promise to him.

Though it was becoming harder and harder.

"I'm on my way, Mom," she said.

"Well, if you're sure you can fit it into your tremendously busy schedule."

"See you in a few minutes."

Brandi's next call was to Adam. No reason to hold him up waiting on her. There was no way they'd be able to work on a video this evening.

"Just knock on my door when you get home," he said.

Brandi swallowed the lump of frustration rising in her throat as she turned onto her mother's block. Both Erin's and her fiancé's cars were in the driveway so she parked on the street in front of her mother's one-level, ranch-style home.

Peals of laughter from the poor, old widow greeted her as she lugged three bags of supplies inside to find her mom in the living room serving her sister and future brother-in-law coffee and peach cobbler.

No one bothered to relieve her of the heavy bags.

"Well, it's about time." Her mother sipped from a delicate china cup. "I wanted to set up in the dining room, but of course, I couldn't have us working in the dark."

"I'm sure Maurice wouldn't have minded taking care of it for you." Brandi leveled a look in her future brother-in-law's direction.

When Maurice had asked if it would be okay for Wesley to serve as his best man, for her sister's sake, Brandi reluctantly agreed. Maurice and Wesley had become good friends while dating the Collins sisters. They had remained close after her and Wesley's breakup and her ex's subsequent move to Atlanta with his new wife.

Still, Maurice's lack of empathy for her, along with his dictatorial manner where Erin was concerned, rankled Brandi.

"We're trying to pull together a wedding in just a few weeks." Her mother spoke slowly as if she were talking to a moron. "Besides, you can't expect a physician to waste his valuable time screwing in lightbulbs."

Brandi rolled her eyes skyward at the way her mother rhapsodized over Maurice. The Collins matriarch was over the moon her youngest daughter was marrying a doctor and never missed an opportunity to make sure everyone was aware of her future son-in-law's profession.

And for all her bluster about the burden of planning a wedding at the last minute, her mother was truly in her element putting her extraordinary organizational skills to work on the event.

"I've been thinking about balloons as centerpieces at the reception instead of roses." Brandi overheard Erin's excited voice. "My friend Kara had them at her wedding reception, and they were beautiful. She gave me the name of the woman who did them."

"If that's what you want, I can give her a call tomorrow," their mother said.

"Balloons? Sounds tacky to me," Maurice said. "We should definitely go with the roses."

"Oh, okay." Erin's voice sounded deflated.

Brandi bit the inside of her mouth. Hard.

Just when she calmed herself down, she overheard Erin telling her mother she wanted to add a pink accent to the red and white theme of the wedding.

"How about we add a few pink carnations to your and Brandi's bouquets? We could also alternate the red velvet bows on the church pews with sweetheart pink ones," Jolene suggested.

"Oh, that will look so pretty," Erin agreed.

Brandi didn't have to wait long for Maurice, not to suggest or ask, but to tell her sister what they were going to do.

"Let's stick with the red and white," he said. "It's more classy."

"You're right, honey," Erin agreed.

None of your business, Brandi silently chanted to herself through gritted teeth. She dumped the bags in the kitchen before heading out to the garage to retrieve the ladder and her father's old toolbox. She slid her hand over the beat-up metal box he took to work every day on construction jobs, before picking it up.

With her dad's final request of her in mind, Brandi squared her shoulders and sucked in a calming breath before returning inside the house, ladder and tools in tow.

She was on the ladder screwing the frosted-glass cover back over the light fixture when she heard Maurice call out to her.

"I've got my eye on the last piece of cobbler, speak up if you want it," he said.

"Goodness, no, Doctor. The last thing Brandi needs is

pie," Jolene Collins chimed in before she could reply. "I've already had to buy her a larger maid-of-honor dress, and I don't want her bursting out of it."

A red-hot flush of mortification stung Brandi's cheeks at the words. God, she hoped the extra sessions she'd booked with Heather made her mother have to eat those very same words.

Three hours later, Brandi dumped the dirty air filters she'd replaced in the trash and checked off the last item on the list. Her mother continued to preside over wedding planning, only breaking to add an additional task to Brandi's list.

"Well, that's everything," Brandi said to the trio. Finally.

Between work and her handyman duties, she was beat. All she wanted was to crawl into bed, pull the covers over her head and stay there until her alarm went off tomorrow morning.

"Brandi, did you take a look at the ceiling fan in my bedroom yet? It's been wobbling."

"Ceiling fan?" She scanned the list again. "This is the first I've heard of it."

"Well, there's definitely something wrong with it. Go see for yourself."

"Mom, it's been a long day."

Her mother put down the guest list she and Erin had been reviewing. "You're already here. It won't take you a minute to check it out for me."

"It's January. You won't even need it for a few months."

"Now how would you feel if it fell off the ceiling right on top of my head?"

A thought flashed through Brandi's mind she'd have to beg forgiveness for in her prayers tonight. She bit down on her tongue as she trudged outside to the garage to retrieve the ladder she'd just put away.

"What happened?" Adam asked, taking in the sight at his front door.

The bubbly Brandi, who had left his place last night eager to begin working on the video for the Lina Todd application, had been replaced by a woman who looked like she was about to drop on the spot.

"I got caught up at my mom's and couldn't get out of there." Brandi stifled a yawn with her fist. "I'll just have to send in the application as is and hope for the best. Sorry I kept you waiting for nothing."

Something about her defeated demeanor tugged at his insides, and he was tempted to write a check to get her handbag business into any retail space she desired. Plus, he was pretty sure he could also pull enough strings to have Lina Todd contact her within the week.

Instead, he glanced at his watch. "We still have three hours until midnight."

It would be wrong just to hand everything to Brandi, he thought, no matter how badly he wanted to. He'd only end up depriving her of a huge sense of accomplishment, and she'd never feel like her success was truly her own. That, he knew from experience.

"Adam, I appreciate the effort, but I'm barely coherent. All I want to do is sleep."

"Sleep is overrated." He grasped her shoulders and turned her in the direction of her front door.

"What are you doing?"

"You're going home, where you're going to revive your-self with a shower and apply whatever magical potions women use on their faces to make them look as if they've had eight hours of sleep," he said. "Meanwhile, I'm walking over to Jolt's to get you an espresso."

"But…" Brandi began, until Adam cut her off.

"If you have energy left to argue, then you have enough to see this project through," he said.

She shot him a withering look. "Okay. I'll shower and get ready," she grumbled. "Hope Jolt's makes one helluva espresso."

After she was inside her condo, Adam stared at her closed door and wondered if he weren't the one who needed a strong drink to clear his head.

What difference should it make to him if she wanted to scrap the video and go to bed?

Right now, his mind should be on the chocolate fig and pistachio sponge cake he planned to attempt tomorrow or reviewing the diagram of the competition kitchen he'd received in an email attachment earlier this evening.

Not on a coffee run.

Twenty minutes later, he watched a decidedly perkier Brandi pace the length of her living room. She'd changed into black velvet pants and a silky top in a flattering shade of green. A hint of strategically placed makeup gave her pretty face just the right amount of color.

She halted midpace and took a second sip from the small paper cup of espresso.

"Wow!" Her brown eyes widened and her brows nearly shot up to her hairline. "This is going to keep me awake for days instead of hours."

"We'll worry about that after we get your application submitted," he said. "Ready?"

Her teeth sank into her bottom lip. "I don't mean to keep making excuses, but the truth is I haven't come up with a concept for the video yet. I barely had time to breathe today, let alone think."

"Don't worry," Adam soothed. "After your second text, I drove down to the spot you intend to lease and shot some footage we can incorporate."

"You did that for me?" Her eyes brightened in surprise. "Thank you."

He shrugged. "It's no big deal."

Too bad he couldn't shrug off the rush of pleasure he felt at knowing he'd pleased her. What was it about this woman? She had him acting like a dog standing on its hind legs for a pat on the head.

Adam cleared his throat. "How about we go into your office and get started?"

He took some preliminary footage of her workspace making sure to zero in on several of the completed handbags. He hoped the camera's zoom feature caught the workmanship and attention to detail she put into the finished product.

"You ready?" he asked.

Brandi, who was sitting behind her desk, nodded at the camera. However, her face looked like the color had been drained out of it.

"Um, hi, I'm, uh…" she stammered.

He paused the video. "How about we start over?" he asked. "Ready?"

Again, she nodded.

"Hi, I'm Bandi Crollins. I'm mean, Crandi Bollins."

Adam stared at her over the camera's LCD screen trying not to laugh. "Crandi, huh?"

"If you haven't figured it out yet, I'm really nervous," Brandi said before collapsing into a fit of giggles.

He put the camera down on her cutting table and crossed the room. Reaching across the desk, he took her hands in his.

"They're ice cold," he said.

"It's just nerves."

He rubbed her hands between his to warm them up. "Close your eyes."

She flashed him a skeptical look.

"Come on, close them. Now take a deep breath and relax." He waited until she complied. "Forget about the camera. All I want you to do is tell me about Arm Candy Handbags, just like you did the other night. Can you do that for me?"

Brandi nodded, her eyes still closed.

"All right then, open your eyes and let's try it again." He reluctantly released her warmed hands, fighting the impulse to bring them to his lips and kiss her fingertips.

He retrieved the camera for another take. His subject looked into the lens and smiled.

"Hi, I'm Brandi Collins, owner of Arm Candy Handbags."

He spent the next half hour following her around her home office with the camera as she explained the ins and outs of her business. Her earlier jitters were replaced with an easy confidence and passion for what she did, which increased as she spoke. It was evident to him tonight, just as it had been the first time she'd showed him her headquarters, Arm Candy was a thriving business long overdue for expansion.

"I believe we have enough." He popped the flash memory card out of the camera.

"So how did I do?"

"You did a great job. I don't think Lina Todd will find a better candidate to personally mentor," he said truthfully. "Now all we have to do is upload the footage and edit it."

Brandi smiled. "I'm lucky you're so tech savvy," she said, "because I don't know a thing about editing video."

Adam froze. "Then we really do have a problem this

time, because neither do I." He glanced at his watch. "We only have an hour and a half to figure it out."

Brandi swiped a hand over her face. "I don't know what we're..." She snapped her fingers. "Lynn."

"Who?"

"She's a friend. She teaches computer science at my high school. She also designed Arm Candy's website." Brandi lifted the receiver off her office phone. "Cross your fingers she's still awake."

Adam looked on as Brandi briefly explained their dilemma to her friend over the phone. As they talked, he could literally see the tension in her shoulders dissipate. She held her hand over the receiver's mouthpiece and looked up at him.

"She'll do it, but is insisting on a chocolate bribe from your kitchen. Please tell me you have something."

"Will chocolate soufflé cake do?"

"Abso-freaking-lutely!" Adam heard Lynn's enthusiastic whoop through the phone's tinny speakers.

After a brief stop by his place to pick up the cake, they headed to the building's parking garage. "I'll drive," Adam volunteered.

"Are you sure? It might be faster if we take my car since I know where we're going."

Adam pressed the button on his key fob, walked over to the passenger side of his black Porsche Cayenne and opened the door. She stared at the luxury SUV and back at him.

"The clock is ticking," he reminded her.

After she was seated, he placed the cake box in the backseat and pulled out of the garage.

"Make a right here, get on I-65 and head south," she directed.

They rode in silence a few moments, before Brandi

spoke again. "I've never been in a Porsche before," she said. "So what exactly did you do at that household-goods company?"

"I was a vice president," Adam said, still not ready to divulge his family ties.

"That explains it."

"Explains what?"

"Why those close to you are so upset," she said. "They're probably thinking you're crazy to turn your back on the kind of salary you must have been pulling down."

"And what do you think?" He braced himself for her answer as he steered the SUV down the expressway. Not that it mattered what she thought, he told himself.

"I guess I'm in your grandmother's camp," she said. "I think you should do what makes you happy."

Adam thought about her reply as he followed Brandi's directions. The more he got to know her, the more he found to like about this woman.

He took the exit ramp off the expressway and eventually pulled into a free parking space in front of a corner-unit town house.

"You'll like Lynn and her husband, James," Brandi said, as they walked up the pathway leading to the door. "They're good friends."

Adam nodded; her reassurance made him feel better about crashing a stranger's place at this time of night. He was further assured by the friendly smiles that greeted him at the door.

"Adam Ellison, meet Lynn and James Myers."

A short woman with flashing amber eyes stepped past a burly man Adam assumed was her husband and grabbed the cake box.

"Nice to meet you, Adam. I'll just take this off your

hands." She lifted the box to her nose and inhaled. "Oh, my God, this smells like heaven."

Brandi confiscated the cake from her friend's hands and passed it off to James. She handed Lynn the camera's memory card.

"Video first, then cake."

"Oh, okay," Lynn grumbled. "Follow me to the computer room, and we'll get started."

She shot her husband a warning glance. "That cake is a bribe for me, not you. So there had better be some left when we're done."

"Well, I suggest you be very efficient at your job," James said.

As the ladies disappeared into another room, James balanced the cake box with one hand and stuck out the other. "In case you missed it in the chocolate-loving whirlwind that's my wife, I'm James."

Adam shook his hand. "Adam. I'm Brandi's next-door neighbor."

James gestured for Adam to follow him as he cut a path through the living room, where the imprints of someone's bottom indented the well-worn sofa and Titans football highlights blared from the flat-screen television, to a small kitchen.

"Oh, I know who you are."

The words took Adam by surprise. His father had always been the public face of Ellison Industries. One would have to scour business-trade magazines to recognize him, Kyle or their uncle.

"You do?"

James grunted. "You're the guy who's got Lynn bugging me about serving her chocolate."

Adam laughed as relief washed over him. "Didn't mean to make you look bad in front of the wife, man."

"Now I'm eager to see what the fuss is all about." James sat the box on the kitchen table and opened it. "What kind of cake is this again?"

"A chocolate soufflé cake."

James retrieved a knife. "Want a piece?"

Adam shook his head. "You go ahead. I've been up to my elbows in chocolate all day."

James cut himself a hunk that could have easily served three people and took a huge bite. Adam waited for an unsolicited opinion as the big man slowly chewed.

He watched as his host rolled his eyes and groaned. "Holy moly!" he exclaimed. "This is the best cake I've ever tasted."

"James Myers!" A high-pitched voice called from the other side of the town house's first floor. "You aren't hogging up all the cake, are you?"

"Aren't you on a diet?" James bellowed. He grabbed a plate from the kitchen cabinet and plunked his slab of cake on it. He turned to Adam. "Can I get you a beer or something?"

"Just a soda if you have it."

James tossed him a cola and inclined his head toward the living room. "You follow the Titans? I was just rewatching some highlights from last Sunday's Wildcard game."

He sat down on the sofa and Adam seated himself in the adjacent armchair; both seats offered a good view of the television.

"It was a good one, wasn't it?" Adam launched into a recap of the team's starting running back's explosive run that resulted in the game-winning touchdown. "I still can't believe they're in the playoffs."

"Man, I'm pinching myself," James said around a huge bite of cake. He polished off the rest of it in two big bites as they watched the game highlights. "So how'd you learn to bake like this?"

"My grandfather owned a bakery," Adam said. "I picked it up from him."

"What do you do?"

"I used to be in business, but I recently got out of it to focus on baking with chocolate," Adam said. "You?"

"Firefighter," he answered. "And I don't know what you put in that cake, but it has to be the best thing I've ever eaten. You should definitely be baking for a living."

Before Adam could thank him, Brandi appeared in the living room.

"I think we're done with the video," she said, "but I'd like you to come take a look at it first."

"Want me to pause the highlight package?" James asked, his eyes never leaving the big-screen television.

"No, you go ahead. I've seen them already."

Adam rose from his seat and followed Brandi into the Myerses' computer room. A long desk, bearing two desktop computers, extended the length of one of the room's four walls. The rest of the room was crowded with boxes. Brandi had mentioned the couple were newlyweds, and their town house looked like they were still working toward merging their belongings.

Lynn Myers vacated her office chair when they walked in.

"Have a seat." She offered him her chair. "We're eager to hear what you think."

Reaching past him, she clicked the mouse and started the video.

Brandi's image filled the large monitor as she introduced herself and her business. Adam watched as the raw footage he'd shot earlier unfolded into a slick, polished piece worthy of a Madison Avenue advertising firm.

It ended with a zoom shot of Arm Candy's logo before fading to black.

"I think it's awesome," he said honestly and then caught a glimpse of the time on the computer screen. "I also think we had better get to Overnight Express. We're already going to have to speed to make it in time."

Lynn made a DVD copy of the video for them to mail, and then they began to say their good-nights.

The Myerses' warmheartedness stuck with Adam as he steered his SUV away from their town house and in the direction of the Overnight Express office.

"You have nice friends," he said into the vehicle's dark cabin illuminated only by the glow of the dashboard's lights.

He caught Brandi's smile in his peripheral vision. "They're pretty cool," she agreed. "She and James got out of their bed to come get me late one night when my car stalled, and the auto club said there would be a two-hour wait."

Adam wondered if Brandi knew just how fortunate she was to have people like the Myerses in her corner.

He'd spent the drive to the delivery service trying to remember the last time someone did him a favor without expecting something in return.

Chapter 9

Brandi's backside burned as if someone had set it on fire.

Positioned on her hands and knees on the hardwood floor of Heather's studio she eked out the last of fifty butt lifts.

"Done." She collapsed with a whoosh at her trainer's sneaker-shod feet.

"Good job, now give me fifty more."

"You've got to be joking."

"Do I look like a comedian?"

Brandi's gaze traveled from Heather's pink Nikes upward to her crossed arms before landing on her unsmiling face. During their workout time, her sweet, funny friend transformed into the lean, mean military hard-ass who had once put fear in the hearts of the country's enemies.

"But I didn't even eat any chocolate yet," Brandi grumbled, pulling herself back onto her hands and knees.

Heather pointed to the big sign hanging on the only

wall of her workout studio not covered in floor-to-ceiling mirrors. "Tell me again, what's the first rule of training?"

"No whining," Brandi said, not bothering to look at the two words inscribed on the sign in bold, black lettering. "But it's not fair."

"Fair? Is it fair you live next door to a fine piece of chocolate-making man candy?" Heather snorted. "And the worst part of it is, you don't even want him."

Oh, she wanted him, all right. Brandi hoisted an achy leg in the air. However, she only allowed herself to have him in her dreams. Dreams that made her blush a little inside every time she saw him.

Brandi paused. "So let me get this straight. You're making me suffer for chocolate and a man I haven't had."

"If you stop, I'm going to lose count and you'll have to start all over again," Heather said, and Brandi resumed the torturous exercise. "I'm making you suffer for the chocolate you're going to have as well as making sure you fit into your maid-of-honor dress."

"Deep down I realize I hired you to do this to me, but the rest of my body can only think about the hell you're putting it through," Brandi said. "What number am I on anyway? Forty-eight? Forty-nine?"

"Keep going, twenty-nine, thirty, thirty-one." Heather plopped down on the floor and sat cross-legged, facing her. "Since you have no interest in the hunk next door, how about giving me an introduction?"

No!

The word didn't get past her clenched teeth, but her strong visceral reaction to her trainer's request caught Brandi off guard. Two kisses didn't make Adam her man. He was a free agent who would probably be thrilled an attractive woman like Heather was interested in him, and jump at the chance to get to know her.

Brandi liked Heather. She liked Adam, too.

Then why did the idea of two people she thought were great getting together bother her so much?

She met Heather's gaze, the corner of her friend's mouth quirked upward in a half smirk.

"Don't bother answering the question," Heather said. "The expression on your face tells me everything I need to know. Your hunk next door is off-limits."

"He's not *my* hunk. I barely know the man."

Heather chuckled as she stood up. "That's why you looked like you wanted to kick my ass."

This time it was Brandi's turn to snort. "I do, but for all of these dang butt lifts. I had to have hit fifty by now."

"Actually, you're up to seventy, but don't go passing out on me yet." Heather retrieved a pair of eight-pound dumbbells from the weight rack. "Let's go to work on those biceps and triceps."

Brandi blew out a breath. The dumbbells felt triple their weight to her push-up-ravaged arms.

"Come on," the trainer coaxed. "You want Wesley to take one look at you and regret how dirty he did you, right?"

Brandi waited for the pangs of anger or bitterness to hit her as she hefted the weights into a set of hammer curls. Both emotions were still there, however, neither packed the powerful punch they had merely a week ago.

The observation wasn't lost on Heather.

"Hmm, looks like I'll have to find a new sore spot to poke. I'm not seeing the fury your ex's name usually evokes."

"It's here."

"Maybe, but it's not the same." Heather rubbed at her chin as she walked a full circle around her. "And it's certainly nothing like the reaction I got when I asked you to hook me up with your neighbor."

"Aren't you being paid to train me?" Brandi snapped, more annoyed at how easily her friend could read her. She might as well have written her innermost thoughts on the wall in the same bold lettering as the "no whining" sign.

Heather's eyes lit up and a smug smile tugged at her lips. "Again, your expression tells me everything I need to know."

"And just what do you think you know, smarty pants?"

"I know there's more going on between you and your neighbor than a bit of chocolate tasting, and if there isn't now it's only a matter of time."

Forty-five minutes later, Brandi hobbled down the hallway leading to her front door. She hoped her legs would hold out until she reached the bottle of Tylenol in her medicine cabinet. After she gulped down two with a glass of water, she could crawl to her sofa until the pain reliever worked its magic.

"Stupid Heather and her stupid observations," she grumbled. So what if she was attracted to Adam. She had no intention of acting on it. They were friends. Until she got Arm Candy out of her spare room and into its own boutique, all she had to offer a man was friendship.

The door next to hers opened and the smell of chocolate hit her just as Adam stepped out. His eyes connected with hers, and her pulse picked up its pace.

"Hey, you," he said.

As always, the man made her mouth water more than her favorite dark chocolate espresso truffles. He wore a leather bomber jacket with jeans. The black leather gave him an edgy, bad-boy appeal that made the bad girl in her crave him even more.

I'm the boss of me. I control this attraction, hormones

or whatever it is. It doesn't control me. Brandi silently repeated the mantra in her head.

"Hello," she finally said aloud.

"You coming from boot camp class?"

She glanced down at her sweaty, undoubtedly smelly, body. Isn't this what she wanted just the other day, for him to see her looking her absolute worst? Then why did she wish she had run into him after she'd showered, run a comb through her hair and added a touch of lip gloss?

"Not boot camp. I added some personal training sessions to make up for the chocolate I've committed to eat as part of our deal. It was sheer agony, so I hope it's worth it."

Despite her appearance, he seemed to devour her with his eyes. The knowledge he wanted her turned her on even more.

"I'm off to replenish my stash now, and I promise to give you an experience you won't forget."

"Looking forward to it."

She took a step toward her door in hopes of breaking the hold this man seemed to have on her. Then he touched her arm, a question in his eyes.

The fleece barriers of her shirt and jacket were excellent at blocking the elements, but couldn't stop the delicious shiver shimmying up her arm and all the way down her back.

Brandi didn't know what he wanted, but every cell in her body was already screaming "yes." He cleared his throat, and she swallowed hard in anticipation.

"What's the delivery status of the package we sent to the Lina Todd Foundation?"

"Uh…um…it arrived," she stammered, before her voice took on what she hoped was a businesslike edge.

So much for believing she'd learned her lesson. They were simply neighbors helping each other out—nothing more. That was all she wanted or needed from Adam Ellison.

She needed to get a handle on herself, Brandi thought. Arm Candy was her priority. Not her love life. Or lack of one.

"Great. When do you plan to finish the other applications?"

"This evening."

"Great. What time?"

Brandi shook her head. Until she was sure she had her "Adam crazy" hormones under control, she needed to keep her distance. "I can fill them out myself, but I would like you to look them over before I submit them."

"No problem. Just say when."

"Well, enjoy your evening." This time Brandi did make it through her door and closed it behind her.

She kicked off her sneakers just as her phone vibrated on the coffee table. Lynn's number lit up on the screen. Her friend had taken her seniors on a trip to a photographic exhibit on the history of computers in America at the Frist Center for the Visual Arts, so they'd missed their usual chat over lunch.

"How was the field trip?" Brandi plopped down on the couch and rubbed her sore calf with her free hand.

"Just dandy. Kids viewed a fascinating exhibit. They learned lots. A good time was had by all," Lynn said. "Okay, now that I've told you all about my exciting field trip, I want to hear every detail about…"

"Just stop right there," Brandi cut her friend off. "I've seen, heard and talked about my neighbor enough for one day. So if this call is about him, you might as well hang up right now."

The sound of Lynn's laughter was the last thing Brandi heard before her friend ended the call with a resounding click.

Way to go, smooth talker. Adam shook his head as he walked down the hallway.

He'd been mentally reviewing his grocery list when he'd run into his neighbor and the sight of her knocked him off kilter. The brisk January wind had swept through her hair and left it in tousled waves framing a cosmetic-free face still glowing from her workout.

And what did he do?

Ask her about an application.

When all he really wanted to do was kiss her until they both had to come up for air. Then ask her how long did she honestly think they could continue to ignore this *thing* between them. He wasn't sure what to call it, but its pull grew stronger with every glance, touch and kiss.

Adam couldn't help appreciating the irony of his situation with Brandi.

Women usually pursued him, fawning over his every word in hopes of gaining his attention.

Now he was the one in hot pursuit. And not getting very far.

Adam steered his SUV out of the building's parking garage onto the street. He'd intended to go directly to the specialty market, but decided to make a detour to his friend Zeke's.

He could use another perspective on the Brandi dilemma, and after their blowup, talking to Kyle was out of the question. Besides, his tennis partner had been missing in action these days, and he needed to find out what was going on with him.

There had been no answer when he'd called to tell Zeke

he was on the way over, but the wrought-iron gates in front of the drive leading to the Holden estate were open.

With its solo McMansion surrounded by two acres of land, the Holden estate was minuscule in comparison to the two stately homes Adam's father had built on twenty acres of land south of the city.

Adam drove through the open gates. He spotted Zeke's red BMW X6 Roadster parked in the circular driveway at the front of the house and pulled his Cayenne behind it. He was surprised to see his friend's prized sports car outside of the garage. Zeke reserved it for dates with women he really wanted to impress. His friend's day-to-day ride was an Escalade.

Kyle had said a Napoleon complex compelled Zeke, who was only five foot six, to drive the big SUV.

Adam didn't agree with his brother's assessment, or his view on Zeke being a hater who was secretly envious because his family's company didn't come close to matching the Ellison conglomerate.

Zeke was under constant pressure from his father to grow their company. As the oldest, Adam knew what it felt like to carry that weight and could empathize more than Kyle.

Adam shut off the Cayenne's engine. He got out of his SUV just as Zeke emerged from the house. Zeke was dressed in his custom suit made by a Hong Kong tailor and reeking of a woodsy cologne his friend insisted drove women wild.

"Hey, man, long time, no see," Adam said.

Zeke froze and stared at him like the proverbial deer caught in oncoming headlights.

"Been working," Zeke finally said, averting his gaze. "Uh, sorry about missing our games the last couple of weeks."

"It's cool. I know what kind of effort goes into running a company. Just let me know when it's a good time for you."

"Yeah, I'll do that."

Adam got the feeling he was making Zeke uncomfortable, but he shook it off. They'd both been busy lately.

"So how's the baking going?" Zeke asked. "You haven't changed your mind about it?"

"No regrets. In fact, I wish I'd done it years ago."

His answer brought a smile to Zeke's face, and he slapped Adam on the back. "Best of luck with it, man."

"Thanks," Adam replied, both surprised and grateful for his friend's support. "So who's the lucky lady this evening?"

Zeke's smile vanished and his expression regained a cagey edge. "Oh, no one you'd know."

"You sure? Our world is a small one," Adam joked. And it was. They'd all grown up alongside each other attending the same private schools, Jack & Jill and ritzy summer camps. Only Adam hadn't participated in the summer camps with Kyle, Zeke and the rest of the kids in their crowd, instead spending the summer months with his grandparents in France.

Zeke made a point of checking the chunky platinum watch on his wrist. "I'd better be going."

Adam nodded. "Take it easy, playa."

"See you around."

Adam got back into his SUV and followed Zeke's BMW through the iron gates. He realized he'd just been blown off. *But why?*

When he arrived at the market, Adam grabbed a handcart near the store's entrance and headed in the direction of the European chocolate aisle for his preferred Belgian brand. His trip over to Zeke's had posed more questions than it answered.

Why had his friend been avoiding him? And who was his mystery woman?

Not to mention, Zeke had been zero help on the Brandi front, but Adam had already decided on his next move.

He'd simply give her space.

Space to figure out what he already knew. Distance wouldn't stem their simmering sexual attraction. It would only fuel it.

Chapter 10

Brandi looked up from her microwaved diet meal to find Lynn standing over her wearing a frown.

"I thought you had lunchroom duty this week," Brandi said.

"Managed to switch days with Madeline so I could corner you." Her friend plunked a salad on the table and sat down in the chair across from her. She raised an inquiring brow.

Brandi knew what her friend wanted the scoop on, but there was nothing to tell.

"I'm a patient woman, but it's been a while now, and you've barely mentioned the hunk of dark chocolate living next door to you."

Brandi rolled her eyes. Restless nights of inhaling chocolate and dreaming about Adam had left her exhausted and crabby. Each night the aroma of chocolate grew stronger and her dreams more explicit. Last night, she'd been tempted to make another middle of the night appearance at his door—only this time to turn her dreams into sheet-sizzling reality.

"I've been keeping a low profile," Brandi said.

Two weeks had passed since she'd found herself on the verge of throwing herself at him in the corridor. Since then Brandi had taken care to avoid Adam. When she'd completed the other microloan applications, she'd slid them under his door with a note attached asking him to look them over.

He'd reviewed the paperwork, made detailed notations and returned it the very same way.

However, her strategy of avoidance had backfired, and at this point, Brandi didn't know what she ached for more—*chocolate or him.*

"How long do you think you can keep it up?" Lynn asked, poking at a cherry tomato with her fork. "You can't steer clear of a next-door neighbor forever."

"Actually, I'm seeing him after work. He's narrowed down his top contenders for the competition, and I'm going to his place to taste test them," she said. "Adam's completed his part of our bargain, now it's my turn."

"Lucky you. James and I almost came to blows over the last slice of his chocolate soufflé cake."

Brandi shrugged; the dispassionate gesture belied the swarm of butterflies knocking around in her stomach. She gave up the pretense of eating and pushed her barely touched meal aside.

"It's just…"

She started to confide in her friend, when the history and biology teachers walked into the small lounge and sat down at a table within earshot. The two men were the biggest gossips in the entire school. Their tongues had wagged so much after her near-wedding to Wesley, she thought they would actually fall out of their mouths.

She and Lynn immediately adopted a covert version of normal conversation they used whenever the two busybodies were around. Fortunately, they'd been friends long enough to comprehend the meaning behind the dropped sentences and exaggerated facial expressions.

"You stressed over calories?" Lynn asked.

Calories were her main concern the first time she'd gone over to his place. Now she only hoped to make it through the evening with her panties intact.

Brandi shook her head slowly, and her friend nodded as understanding dawned.

"So you want to?"

"Desperately," she admitted with a sigh.

"But?"

"I'm this close to getting Arm Candy where I want it," she said in a voice low enough hopefully only Lynn could hear. "I don't want to get caught up in *you know* and lose my focus."

"Who says you have to get caught up?"

Brandi mouthed the word, "What?"

The buzz of conversation at the next table came to an abrupt halt, but the nosy teachers next to them weren't eating. Lynn gave them the side eye and then looked at Brandi.

"You done?"

Brandi nodded. They rose from the table, tossed out their picked-over lunches and exited the lounge.

"When is the last time you had fun?" Lynn asked.

Brandi turned the question over in her head, but couldn't come up with an answer. When *was* the last time she enjoyed herself? Flashes of purple roses, being handfed cake, long conversations about aspirations and grandmas and kisses sweeter than the finest milk chocolate played through her mind.

The fact Adam was a part of the best moments she'd experienced in a very long time wasn't lost on her. If she didn't know better, she'd think she was falling in...

No, she was being silly. She couldn't be. She refused to even think the word.

"I'm not saying you should fall in love." Her friend said the word instead. "But if I were you, I wouldn't pass up an opportunity to fall into his bed."

Brandi spent the remaining four hours at work teaching art as the words Adam had said to her the night they met rang in her ears. The same ones he whispered against her ear every night in her dreams.

"Stop trying to resist the irresistible."

Brandi shook her head hard as if it would exorcise him from her brain. She didn't know how she was going to do it but somehow she had to get a rein on herself before she saw him again.

Adam wasn't sure if his strategy of giving Brandi space had made a difference in her feelings, but it sure as hell was doing a number on him.

He missed looking at her. He missed talking to her. He missed the honey-sweet taste of her lips.

He missed *her*.

Adam glanced at the microwave clock as he added delicate shards of dark chocolate to the dome of the chocolate sponge cake filled with a creamy bitter chocolate mousse. Brandi would be here soon. He wanted this, as well as the two other cakes he'd prepared for her to sample today, to be perfect.

He didn't know why; after all, he'd only known her a short while, but a small part of him wanted to impress her nearly as much as he did the competition's international panel of judges.

"You're being an idiot," he said, carefully placing the last sliver of chocolate atop his creation.

Time had only strengthened the woman's resolve to keep their relationship strictly platonic, and he would be smart to do the same. He needed to focus on winning the competition, not trying to win Brandi Collins.

A knock sounded at the door and his groin tightened at the thought of her on the other side of it. So much for maintaining focus.

He wiped his hand on a tea towel and blew out a breath. She was there to eat cake, he reminded himself. Nothing more.

Adam opened the door and drank in the sight of her. She'd eschewed the beat-up sweats she'd worn on her last visit, in that ineffective attempt to turn him off. Instead, a knee-skimming black skirt showcased her shapely calves while a pink sweater accented luscious curves he longed to take his time exploring—first with his hands, and then with his mouth.

"So what have you got for me this evening?" She slid her tongue over her glossed lips in what was probably an innocent gesture, but it left him rock hard.

"Cakes." The hoarse word was all he could push past the lump lodged in his throat.

"Well, what are we waiting for?" she asked. He swallowed hard and willed himself not to explode in his pants. "I've been exercising like a madwoman," she continued, "so I plan to enjoy every sinful mouthful."

"Come in and we'll get started," Adam said, grateful for the return of the bass in his voice and that his black chef's apron helped conceal his aroused state.

He closed his eyes as she walked past him and silently

prayed for fortitude. Instead, he caught the alluring scent of her orange-blossom-and-gardenia-infused perfume.

This was going to be a long evening.

"Wow!" He heard her exclaim from the dining room, where he'd already placed the first cake.

A combination of rich mousse and fluffy meringue, it was the lightest of the three cakes he made for her first round of tasting. He'd decorated the chocolate ganache topping with a cluster of chocolate leaves he'd fashioned by brushing the veined side of fresh lemon leaves with a thin layer of chocolate. After the chocolate set, he peeled it away from each leaf and transferred the delicate chocolate foliage to the refrigerator to cool before arranging it on the cake.

"You can't possibly expect me to eat this." She stared at the cake, a look of awe on her face. "It's too beautiful."

No, you're beautiful, he thought. "You have to eat it. We had a deal, remember?"

"Is this the only one you want me to try?"

Adam shook his head. "I thought we'd start off with this one. I have two more in the kitchen. I'll go get them," he said.

This time he was the one stepping away from her, hoping a few moments of distance would cool him off.

In the kitchen, Adam slid his hand down over his face in frustration. How in the hell was he supposed to concentrate on cake with a raging hard-on and everything about the woman in the next room exciting him even more?

He was a man who prided himself on always being in control, but this whole thing was getting out of hand, he thought, bracing his palms on the edge of the stainless-steel stove. Forget their deal. The best course of action was to march out there and let Brandi off the hook.

Adam spun around to go into the dining room to do

just that, but instead slammed into her. The impact of the collision sent the silverware in Brandi's hands clanging to the floor and her against the kitchen island.

Instinctively, he grabbed ahold of her arms to steady her. Their eyes met and held for a moment.

"You okay? I didn't see you behind me."

She nodded, her backside against the island. "I thought I'd make myself useful by getting the forks."

He looked down at her upturned face. Her lips were slightly parted and he could feel the warmth of her breath.

"Brandi, maybe you should go. My mind isn't on chocolate this evening."

"Neither is mine," she said softly.

"The truth is, all I can think about is how badly I want…"

She silenced him with a brief touch of her fingertips to his mouth.

"Don't tell me," she whispered. "Show me."

Adam swore hoarsely under his breath and clasped a handful of her hair. The thick, glossy curls felt like silk against his fingertips. Pulling her to him, he seized her mouth in a kiss that was both long and deep. Unlike their first brief kiss, he had the luxury of time to savor her sweet taste and the feel of her tongue mingling with his.

She moaned deep in her throat. One of her hands cradled the back of his neck and the other drifted down to his butt, both wrenched him closer until his body was flush with hers. The move made it unmistakably clear. She wanted him just as badly.

He ground his erection against her and she arched forward. Adam could feel her taut nipples against his chest, and he tore his mouth from hers.

As if she sensed his next move, Brandi grabbed the edge of her sweater and pulled it up and over her head. Her hair tumbled down around her shoulders as the discarded garment fell to the floor.

Adam stared down at the red lace bra encasing her breasts and sucked in a sharp breath. He caressed them with his eyes before allowing his hands to touch her bare skin. Aah, satin smooth. Just as he'd imagined it.

Cupping her breasts in his palms, Adam balanced their delicious weight in his hands as he smoothed his thumbs over her beaded nipples. He leaned in and kissed the top of her breasts not covered by the sexy red bra, running the tip of his tongue along the scalloped edge where lace met skin.

God, she tasted good. His hands continued to explore her breasts while his lips kissed a path to the pulse point on her throat he'd spent the last weeks dreaming of putting his mouth on. The sweet spot thumped an erratic beat against his mouth as the intoxicating fragrance of her perfume, mingled with a scent that was uniquely Brandi, consumed him.

"Adam," she gasped.

The sound of his name on her lips cut through the sensual haze enveloping him, and he reluctantly pulled away. He closed his eyes to rally his strength before taking a step backward. His cock twitched in protest at being deprived of her inviting warmth.

"What's wrong?" she asked, her voice husky with desire.

Adam looked from her lace-encased breasts to her face. He held her gaze a moment, and the vulnerability he saw within the depths of her eyes reaffirmed his decision to do right by her.

"Are you certain this is what you want?" he asked. "At this point, we can put the brakes on and go back to being simply neighbors."

There was a beat of silence, which crawled by like hours, before she answered with a nod.

"Say it," he said, wanting to make absolutely sure.

Her eyes never left his face as she reached down and palmed his heavy erection. He locked his knees to keep them from buckling. Just when he didn't think he could get any harder, he did.

"I want you to do what you promised," she demanded.

With little or no blood left in his brain, Adam couldn't recall his own name, let alone what he'd apparently told her.

"Exactly what did I promise?"

Releasing his cock, Brandi leaned back against the edge of the counter and undid the front clasp on her bra. Adam swallowed as he watched her big, beautiful breasts bounce free from their lacy confinement.

His mouth went dry at the sight of the round globes, the areolas surrounding taut nipples darkened by passion. She let the bra straps slip off her shoulders before removing it and flinging it to the floor on top of her discarded sweater.

"You promised—if I came over to taste your chocolate— to give me an experience I wouldn't forget."

Chapter 11

The air left Brandi's lungs with a whoosh as Adam effortlessly picked her up by the waist and deposited her onto the island's granite countertop.

She didn't know a woman alive who didn't want to feel feather-light in a man's arms, and up until now, she'd thought it was an impossibility for her. They'd barely gotten started, and already the man had kept his promise and given her something to cherish forever.

Adam skimmed his hands along Brandi's thighs, causing her skirt to ride up. His fingertips continued their advance until he reached the waistband of her hose.

"Lift," he commanded.

Leaning backward, she braced her hands behind her and did as she was told. She raised her bottom off the countertop allowing him to pull the panty hose down over her hips.

Adam licked his full lips, sending a shudder through her. He slowly peeled the offending stockings off her legs and added them to the growing pile of clothing on the kitchen floor.

Her skirt pushed up around her waist, she watched his gaze zero in on her skimpy bikinis, a perfect match to the red lace bra.

An appreciative gleam lit his dark brown eyes.

"Pretty panties." He stepped between her legs. "I was afraid you'd have on granny panties in one of your attempts to dissuade me."

"And would they have?"

Adam grasped her legs and yanked. Her bottom slid along the smooth countertop until his erection collided with the apex of her thighs.

"Do I feel like a man dissuaded?"

Brandi moaned as excitement dampened her panties at the concrete feel of him. He swallowed her cry with his mouth. The kiss was rough and possessive in contrast to his achingly gentle hands, which kneaded her breasts while his thumbs teased her nipples.

Just when she thought she'd pass out from sheer pleasure, he replaced his thumbs with his mouth. She gripped the back of his head and pulled him closer. However, her urgency didn't hurry him. He languidly sucked her breasts, lavishing each one with rapt attention.

Instinctively, she gyrated her core against his hardness. The exquisite friction made her tingle all over. Layers of cloth still separated their lower bodies, but it felt so good she could come from this contact alone.

He tore his mouth from her breast.

"Oh, no you don't," he said. "If anybody's going to make you come, it's going to be me."

He deftly removed her lace panties and added them to the heap on the floor. The move left her naked, except for the skirt still bunched around her waist. Her thighs were splayed open, but before she could feel self-conscious, he quickly repositioned her. He placed the backs of her knees on his shoulders, leaving her legs dangling over his broad back.

"I know you're supposed to do the tasting tonight, but I can't resist going first."

He leaned in and dropped a kiss to the top of her mound.

"Adam, please," she said, his name a breathless plea.

Brandi heard a growl vibrate low in his throat before he covered her innermost spot with his mouth. It was all she could do not to buck off the counter as he flicked his tongue over her sensitive folds and feasted on her.

He made love to her with his mouth.

His lips.

His tongue.

Each touch, each kiss, each suck and every lick arousing her to heights she didn't know existed. She dropped back onto her elbows, arched her back and pressed her slick, swollen folds against his superbly talented tongue.

Brandi came fast and hard, shouting his name over the shockwaves of the most incredible orgasm she'd ever experienced.

He caught her boneless body before it collapsed on the hard countertop and hugged her close. Brandi melted into him, her arms around his neck and legs wound tightly around his waist.

Tucking a knuckle under her chin, he raised it and grazed her lips with a whisper-soft kiss that tasted of her.

"That was…" Brandi searched her brain for an adjective big enough to describe what they'd just shared and how it made her feel.

"Only the beginning," he finished for her. "I made you a promise, and I fully intend to keep it."

His large hands cupped her bottom and he carried her

out of the kitchen and through the dining room, her body still wrapped around his. He paused in front of a door before kicking it open and striding through it.

Brandi exhaled a deep, satisfied sigh when he laid her in the center of his king-size bed. The plush comforter beneath her felt like she was sinking into a cloud.

He switched on a bedside lamp bathing the room in amber light. While the majority of his place was a decorating work in progress, the bedroom, like his kitchen, was complete.

Brandi soaked in her surroundings. The room reflected the man. The dark wood of the heavy furniture was reminiscent of his smooth, espresso-brown skin, while the faint scent of chocolate she'd forever associate with him clung to his pillow.

"I think we can get rid of this." Adam stood at the edge of the bed and tugged at the hem of her skirt.

Brandi lifted her hips and it shimmied down her body, and he flung it aside. He stared down at her nakedness. Goose bumps erupted on her bare skin under his scrutiny.

"Damn, you're beautiful." His deep voice took on a husky quality, and she had no doubt he meant what he said. Then again, Adam Ellison had proved to be a man who'd never been anything but completely honest. "I could spend hours just looking at you."

Brandi realized she was the only one devoid of clothing. He was still completely dressed, including the black, bibbed apron hanging around his neck.

"I can hardly believe you're finally in my bed." He continued to look at her nude body as if he were committing every inch of it to memory.

"Neither can I," she confided, emboldened by his stark appraisal. She looked over at the wall separating their bedrooms. "Do you know how many times I lay in my bed on the other side of that wall thinking about you?"

"Really?" He sounded surprised.

She nodded. "I came close to knocking on your door in the middle of the night again."

He raised a brow. "What for?"

"To see you without those clothes."

He chuckled and the rich timbre made her core tingle in anticipation. Brandi rose and then leaned back on her elbows to watch as one by one, every item of clothing joined her skirt on the carpet.

The man's nude body was a work of art, and she paid homage to it with her hungry gaze. From his wide shoulders down to his flat abdominals and lower to the massive erection jutting out from between his muscular thighs, the fact he was hers for tonight overwhelmed her senses and flooded her with desire.

Brandi felt the bed dip as he joined her. Immediately, her hands reached out to touch what up until now only her eyes had taken pleasure in. She skimmed eager fingers over his defined chest and broad back, before letting them roam below the waist to his lean hips and taut rear end.

Saving the best for last, she took his steely length in her hand and heard his sharp intake of breath in her ear. The long, thick feel of him shoved her first orgasm into the distant past, and all she could think about was her next one.

"If you keep touching me like that, this is going to be over before it starts," he warned.

"I want you inside me," she said, squirming on the bed, "now."

Adam reached between them and brought the hand wrapped around him to his lips. Slowly, deliberately, he kissed the tips of her fingers one by one. "So what else did you think about on the other side of that wall in the middle of the night?"

"Please," she begged, wanting what only he could give her. "Don't tease me. I've spent too many nights in bed alone tormented by fantasies of you and chocolate."

He reached past her to retrieve a condom from the nightstand drawer, and she unconsciously licked her lips watching him sheath himself.

Positioning himself over her, he nudged her opening with his incredible hardness and everything female in her clenched in excitement.

"If it's chocolate you want…" He paused. "There's plenty in the kitchen."

The heat of his muscular body surrounded her, and any self-control Brandi had left was trumped by overpowering need. Gripping his behind with her hands, she thrust her hips upward, uniting them.

The hoarse sounds of their collective gasps filled the room.

"God, you feel good," he rasped.

"Oh, yeah," Brandi said breathlessly. "This is the chocolate I've craved all along."

Adam surged forward, deeper. "Then I'll make sure it's the best you've ever had."

It was after midnight when Adam awoke, a sleeping Brandi snuggled deep within his embrace.

He lifted his chin off the top of her head, and peeled his body away from hers. She stirred, but the pull of sleep was too strong.

Gingerly pulling back the comforter, he got out of bed and re-covered her naked body. He fought the urge to let his hands slide over the spectacular curves he'd touched at least a hundred times last night and already committed to memory. He felt himself getting hard again and crossed the room for his robe.

She deserved her sleep, Adam thought. He'd ridden her hard last night, and she'd given as good as she got, matching him stroke for stroke. Her cries of passion still rang in his ears.

What kind of loser would leave a woman like her at the altar? he wondered as he picked her clothes up off the kitchen floor. No doubt her ex would eventually realize his mistake, but it was too late.

Brandi was his now, Adam thought and hoped like hell it was true. That thought brought him to his real reason for not waking her up. He didn't want her to leave. Not yet.

As if she read his mind, Brandi appeared in the bedroom doorway. Her nude body was wrapped in his bedsheet. The vision brought to mind ancient statues of voluptuous goddesses art lovers traveled across Europe to view.

"You're up." He stated the obvious, taking in her tousled hair and kiss-swollen lips.

She had the look of a woman who'd been thoroughly made love to, and he felt honored she'd trusted him with her body.

Now he had to convince her to trust him with her heart.

"I was looking for my clothes," she said. "I'd better be getting back to my place. It's past midnight, and my alarm goes off at five."

"You can't go yet."

"But it's a school night." She lifted a brow and a smile tugged at the corner of her mouth. "And thanks to you, I'm exhausted."

"Too tired for cake?"

Her eyes widened, and her face lit up like a kid who'd been offered keys to a candy store. "I think I can stay a bit longer," she said. "Just let me get dressed, and I'll meet you in the kitchen."

Adam ate up the distance between them in two long strides. He picked her up caveman-style and tossed her over his shoulder.

"Oh, my God! What are you doing?" She giggled as she kicked her legs and pummeled his back with her fists. "Put me down."

He gave her a playful smack on her backside. "Don't fight me, woman."

Adam strode back into the bedroom and dropped her onto the sex-rumpled bed. "Lay back and make yourself comfortable while I round up the cakes."

"But my clothes?"

"Are off-limits until further notice."

He returned with a tray with two of the cakes he'd intended for her to taste before they were sidetracked, accompanied by a tall glass of water and a saucer of unsalted water crackers to cleanse her palate between bites. Brandi was sitting up in his bed leaning against a cluster of pillows, the sheet wrapped enticingly around her breasts and tucked under her arms.

She smiled as he walked in the room, and his heart split open with a burst of sheer adoration.

"I hope you're not going to worry yourself over calories," he said.

Brandi rubbed her hands together as she stared at the cake-laden tray. "Just this once, I'm not going to fret over a single one," she said. "I've been working out like a maniac for weeks waiting on this, so I plan to enjoy every bite guilt free."

"I know I told you there would be three cakes, but you distracted me, and my timing was off on the lava cake and I want you to experience it fresh from the oven," he said.

"Believe me, I'm not feeling deprived." She made a grab for a fork, but he put his hand over it.

"Not yet, sweetheart." The endearment slipped out before he could catch it. "First, let me tell you about each one."

She fell back against the headboard in a huff, folding her arms over her chest. Her lips poked out in a pout that made him want to kiss them.

Adam dragged his attention away from her sexy mouth and tried like hell to keep his focus on cake.

He blew out a breath before he began filling her in on the details of the competition.

"While the professional chefs compete in five divisions including one with an extravagant showcase cake, self-taught chefs are only required to present two plated desserts," he explained. "These are the final candidates for my second dessert. You've already helped me perfect the first one."

"I didn't have much choice. You practically accosted me in the hallway."

"I don't remember you putting up much of a fight." He grinned.

She reached inside his robe and raked her nails lightly over his chest. "Maybe I just can't resist the irresistible."

Adam covered her hand with his, not wanting to lose the warmth of her touch just yet. "And am I irresistible?"

She nodded. "And after last night you can add insatiable to the list."

He glanced at the sheet, barely covering her lush breasts and his cock stiffened. "You're making it extremely difficult for me to keep my mind on the competition."

"Speaking of which," Brandi said, "you never told me what prize the winner receives."

Adam ran down the list of prizes including the magazine articles, Food Network stint and cash.

"A quarter of a million dollars." She bolted upright on the bed, pulling her hand away from his chest. "Holy moly! With that kind of money, you could start the biggest, best chocolate pastry shop in town. No wonder you're putting everything on the line."

He opened his mouth to tell her the money wasn't a big deal. The other prizes were more important to him, along with the validation winning the competition would bring.

Instead, he let the opportunity to fill her in on his background pass. The truth of it was he liked the way she looked at him and simply saw a man.

Not a millionaire.

Not a power-wielding vice president of a major corporation.

Just him. *The real him.*

"Well, what are you waiting on?" Brandi asked impatiently. "Bring on the cake." She lightly poked a finger at his chest. "We've got a competition to win."

Adam cut into the first cake with the side of the fork and held the bite out to her.

"Keep it up, you'll spoil me," Brandi said. "I'll expect men to hand-feed me all the time."

"You deserve to be spoiled," he said.

She wrapped her mouth around the fork, took the bite of cake and chewed slowly.

"Mmm," she moaned and threw her head back. The positively indecent sound and her blissful expression were identical to what he'd heard and saw hours ago when she'd straddled his hips and rode him to her third orgasm of the night.

Willing his cock not to rise, he pushed the delicious memory aside and focused on describing the cake.

"You're eating a chocolate almond sponge cake filled with bitter chocolate mousse, over a layer of crispy praline and topped with shards of dark chocolate."

"Keep in mind, I haven't had one iota of training in judging chocolate or desserts," Brandi cautioned.

"I know." Adam nodded. "But your suggestion to add espresso to the ganache of the triple chocolate cake was right on target. I respect your opinion. Just tell me what you like or don't like."

She inclined her head toward the cake. "The intricate pattern on the sponge is remarkable. It must have taken you hours."

"The French call the decorative designs baked into the sponge a *joconde imprime*," Adam said. "This one is good, but pales in comparison to the ones my grandfather used to create."

"So what will the judges be looking for?"

"Taste will account for eighty percent of the score rounded out by five percent each for texture and after-taste with the remaining ten percent of the score dedicated to overall impression."

Brandi ate a few of the crackers and took a sip of water before snatching the fork from his hand.

"No fair trying to influence the judge." She pointed it at him. "You won't be able to manipulate the real judges by feeding them and sexing them up."

"Touché, Mademoiselle Collins."

"Nor will you be able to sway them with your sexy, French sweet talk."

"Okay," Adam relented, holding up his hands in mock surrender. "I'll back off."

He was as good as his word. He let her get on with tasting and restricted his comments to telling her what was in the particular cake she was eating.

"The filling of this one consists of layers of milk chocolate mousse and chocolate meringue and it's covered with an espresso dark chocolate ganache."

Brandi chased her second bite of it with a sip of water, then rested her back against the pillows and stared down at the two cakes.

"The first one is very, very good," she began. "When I initially tasted it, I thought nothing could beat it, and then I had a bite of the second one and fell completely in love."

Brandi prodded at the mousse and meringue holding the ultra-thin layers of cake together with the prongs of her fork. "It's the texture. You look at it and expect something dense, but it's so light it practically liquefies in your mouth. Definitely the better of the two."

"I agree, but it lacks complexity. There's something missing," he said. "It's frustrating because I know it's something simple. Maybe I'm too close…"

"What have you tried?"

Adam shrugged. "Citrus, berries, nuts, vanilla."

"Caramel?"

He nodded.

"How many versions have you made?"

"I've lost count. By now I could probably make it in my sleep. This is the best one so far. I added balsamic vinegar to the ganache."

"That explains the wonderful sweet-tart zing to it."

Brandi nibbled at a few crackers to help reset her tastebuds before trying another bite, chewing it even slower than her first ones. He could practically see the wheels of her beautiful brain turning as she rolled the food around in her mouth.

"You're right. I believe your solution is simple," she said. "My first suggestion would be to try it with a pinch of cayenne pepper added to the ganache, or scratch the pepper, and try a lavender-infused balsamic vinegar."

Adam thought about her suggestions. He'd definitely put both to the test later this morning. However, her idea to try lavender-infused vinegar truly intrigued him.

"So what do you think?"

He stood and removed the tray from the bed. He placed it on the bedside table before leaning down and kissing her soundly on the lips. "I think I have a genius in my bed."

"What does this genius have to do to get her clothes back?"

"I don't think that's the question you should be asking yourself," he said.

"Then exactly what should I be asking?"

He untied the belt on his robe. He watched her eyes drop below his waist and zero in on a certain part of his anatomy. It left no doubt he was in no hurry for her to leave.

"Do you even want your clothes?"

She let the sheet covering her luscious body fall away, and he had his answer.

Chapter 12

Brandi spent the next day in hand-to-hand combat with Murphy's Law.

She misplaced her cell phone.

Changed a flat tire in the pouring rain.

Threw a student out of her class for disciplinary problems.

Spilled acrylic paint on her desk.

Yet, she couldn't remember the last time she'd felt so utterly wonderful.

Her mood didn't go unnoticed.

"What happened to you?" Lynn had asked her when she'd run into her in the hallway after their second-period classes.

Brandi knew the rain had decimated her makeup, wrinkled her outfit and left her still-damp hair looking like ode to wet dog, so she'd automatically launched into an account of her car tire blowing out on the way to work.

Her friend had waved off the explanation. "You know good and well what I'm talking about and it's not a tire." Lynn's eyes narrowed. "You did it, didn't you?"

"What?" Brandi had feigned innocence, but couldn't stop the grin she knew had spread across her face as images of Adam's hands and lips touching her everywhere flitted through her head.

If she hadn't had to work today, she would have never left his bed.

"You did!"

"How did you guess? It couldn't be that obvious."

"The smile, the swagger. When I first walked over I could hear you humming," she said. "You might as well be wearing a giant sandwich board emblazoned with the words: *I GOT SOME!*"

Her friend hadn't been the only one.

After work, Brandi had a session with Heather, and while the trainer didn't have Lynn's seemingly clairvoyant talents, she did mention noticing something different.

"I'm the same woman you exercised into the ground less than forty-eight hours ago," Brandi had told her as Heather led her through a series of squats and shoulder presses with eight-pound hand weights.

She thought she'd dodged her trainer's questions and scrutiny when Heather snapped her fingers.

"I know what it is," she'd said. "I don't know how I didn't notice it right off."

"You're imagining things."

"Oh, no I'm not," Heather shot back. "I worked you extra hard today, yet you haven't whined or complained once. Instead, you're smiling."

Fortunately, their session ended before Heather, too, figured it out.

By the time Brandi pushed open the stairwell door on

her floor of her condo building, she almost believed she was carrying a sign. She was so deep in thought, she didn't see the well-muscled arm reach out for her as she passed Adam's doorway until it was too late.

"So you thought you were just going to sneak past my door without paying the toll." Her neighbor hauled her against his hard chest.

"A toll?" Brandi laughed. "For using the corridor?"

"That's correct. Now you owe me a kiss."

Before she could protest, he dipped his head and claimed her mouth in a kiss that made her toes curl inside her sneakers. His mouth tasted of mint and he smelled faintly of chocolate. When they finally broke apart, all she wanted him to do was kiss her again.

"Did that cover my toll fee?"

"I'm not sure, let me check." Adam kissed her again, only this time instead of lowering his mouth to hers, he lifted her until her lips were on an even keel with his and her feet dangled above the floor.

Brandi returned the kiss hungrily and basked in the delight of feeling weightless. When it was over, it was all she could do not to wrap her legs around his waist and beg him to take her again.

"Maybe you should put me down now," she said.

"What if I don't want to?"

Brandi squirmed and pressed her palms against his chest. "I'm all sweaty," she said. "Give me time to shower and by the time that molten lava cake is ready, I'll be kicking down your door."

"You're welcome to use my shower." He tightened his arms around her.

"But I don't have any clothes to change into."

"I know." He buried his face in the curve of her neck and began a trail of kisses down her throat. His touch soothed the aches from her workout, and every muscle in her body turned to jelly.

A growl sounded and Brandi plastered her body even closer to his, enjoying the power to bring out the primal side of him.

She heard it again and realized it wasn't a growl at all, but the sound of someone clearing their throat.

"Brandi Louise Collins!"

Brandi flinched at the use of her full name, and her hands fell away from Adam as she turned in the direction of the familiar voice.

"Mom, I…I wasn't expecting you," she stammered. Thirty years melted away in an instant, and Brandi felt like a four-year-old caught in the act of doing something naughty.

"That's obvious." Jolene Collins's disapproving gaze flickered from her daughter to the man holding her.

Brandi pushed her hands lightly against Adam's chest. This time he set her back on her feet and slowly released her from his embrace.

"Mom, this is Adam Ellison. He's my neighbor."

"Hmm." Her mother's eyes narrowed.

Adam stepped forward and extended his hand. "Pleasure to meet you, Mrs. Collins."

Her mother regarded him with a frosty smile and another suspicion-laced, "Hmm," but briefly shook his hand.

She turned to Brandi. "I stopped by to talk to you about Erin's wedding. I've been trying to call you all day. Didn't you get my messages?" Jolene sniffed.

"I lost my cell phone. I've been looking for it all day."

"Where?" Her mother inclined her head toward Adam. "Down his throat?"

Brandi retrieved her key from her jacket pocket and

unlocked her front door, eager to get her mother inside before she embarrassed her any further.

"I'll let you ladies enjoy your visit," Adam said.

"We'd appreciate it, Mr. Ellison." Her mother walked past them into Brandi's condo.

Brandi looked at Adam and mouthed "sorry."

He grabbed her and planted a quick kiss on her lips. "I'll see you later?"

"Definitely."

Brandi stepped through the door just in time to see her mother surveying the refrigerator. If she was looking for anything fattening to rail on her about, she'd be disappointed. The only thing in her fridge was fresh produce.

"So, Mom, what brings you by?"

Jolene closed the refrigerator door and crossed her arms over her chest. "Mind telling me what the spectacle I witnessed in the hallway was all about?"

None of your business. The words sat on the tip of Brandi's tongue along with a reminder that she was thirty-four years old and didn't owe anyone explanations.

However, she was feeling good for the first time in a long while, and she didn't want to dampen her mood with an argument.

"Like I said, we're neighbors. He moved in a few weeks ago."

"You two are pretty friendly to have known each other such a short while."

"We're friends, Mom." Brandi hoped that would be the end of it, but she knew better.

"Your friend is awfully good-looking," Jolene said. "It almost makes you wonder..." Her voice trailed off.

"Why he's kissing me?" Brandi asked aloud, before she could catch herself. "That is what you're asking, isn't it?"

"Don't put words in my mouth, dear. All I'm trying to

say is he looks like the type of man who could have his choice of women."

"And you find it hard to believe he would want me?"

"My God, what's gotten into you? You're so aggressive this evening."

"I apologize if I jumped to conclusions," Brandi said wearily. "You said you wanted to talk about Erin's wedding."

"Oh, yes. I wanted to get an update on your diet," she said. "How much have you lost? I can't tell anything from looking at you."

"Seven pounds."

"That's all? Well, it's a good thing I had the foresight to make sure you have a bridesmaid's dress that fits."

As she had so many times before, Brandi let the dig pass. This was her mother, after all.

"Was there anything else?"

"Are you trying to get rid of me?" Her mother plopped down in a chair at the breakfast bar sending the silent signal that she wasn't leaving until she was good and ready.

"Not at all," Brandi lied. "Would you like a soda or some coffee?"

"No, thanks." The older woman pulled an appointment book from her bag. "I need to double-check the days you plan to take off work for the wedding."

Brandi poured herself a glass of water from her filtered pitcher. "Valentine's Day is on a Wednesday, I have the entire week off plus the Friday before."

"Good, I have everything covered, just in case I need you." Her mother made a notation in the book and slammed it shut. "Now back to that neighbor of yours," she said. "What do you know about him?"

I know he's smart, kind, generous and I enjoy his com-

pany very much. Brandi took a long, slow sip of water, and then answered. "We're just friends, Mom."

"And what does your friend do for a living?"

In a perfect world, Brandi would have told her mother about the big chocolate competition Adam was preparing for and then take her over to his place to sample one of his heavenly creations.

Unfortunately, this was the real world.

"He's between jobs right now, but he's working on something really big."

"I knew it!" Jolene snapped her fingers. "Your mama's no fool, and I knew that man was up to something."

"What are you talking about?"

"I'm talking about the fact that he doesn't have a job."

"He left his job to pursue his dream."

"Does *his dream* bring in a paycheck?" her mother mimicked.

"Not yet, but Adam's very good at what he does and it's just a matter of time." *And I believe in him,* she silently added.

"Humph," her mother snorted derisively. "It's just a matter of time before he starts asking you to loan him money. A car payment here. A rent payment there." Jolene's eyes narrowed. "If he hasn't already."

"Of course not. Adam's not like that and as we both know, I no longer have any money."

"You have a steady job."

Not for long, Brandi thought.

"All I'm saying is after that debacle with Wesley, I'd hate for our family to be publicly humiliated again," she said. "Especially now that your sister's about to become the wife of an up-and-coming physician."

"I told you already, Mom, we're friends."

"For your sake, I hope that's true."

* * *

Adam stared down at the cakes he'd made incorporating Brandi's suggestions, one with lavender-infused balsamic and the other with a pinch of cayenne added to the ganache, but he didn't really see them.

The scene in the hallway replayed through his head with haunting familiarity. An adult child trying to appease an overbearing, disapproving parent.

He remembered Brandi saying she and her mom weren't close, and he hoped things turned out better for them than they had for him and his father.

Not truly knowing his father on a personal level would always be one of his biggest regrets.

Even as Adam eulogized him at the funeral, all he could speak on was David Ellison's business acumen and tireless dedication to Ellison Industries. He hadn't had a single personal anecdote to share with regard to the man lying dead in the flower-topped bronze box.

There'd been none of the father-son baseball games or fishing trips other boys enjoyed with their fathers. It was one of the reasons he and Zeke had bonded so easily as kids. His friend's father was of the same ilk.

A knock on his front door pulled him from thoughts best left in the past. He flung it open expecting to see Brandi.

"Jade," he said.

As always, his ex-fiancée had the salon-fresh look of a woman who spent a great deal of time and money on her appearance. She was dressed in her typical designer ensemble topped by a black suede coat and accessorized with needle-heeled boots and the latest two-thousand-dollar "it" bag.

"Adam." She threw her arms around his neck and kissed him on the mouth. Her lips were flat and lifeless. They felt nothing like the sweet, pliant mouth he'd spent the night before kissing.

The kiss, like her visit, had taken him by surprise, and it took him a moment to recover. He pulled her arms from around his neck and took a step backward.

Unfortunately, he hadn't disentangled himself quickly enough. Brandi's door was open, and her mother was standing in the hallway glaring at him.

His first inclination had been to catch Brandi's mother before she went back inside Brandi's condo to share with her daughter what she thought she'd seen. However, he could only put out one fire at a time, and if Jade was on his doorstep she believed they had some unfinished business.

If that was the case, he wanted to find out what it was and finish it.

"Can we talk?" Jade asked, oblivious to Jolene Collins slamming Brandi's door so hard the entire hallway shook.

Adam nodded and stepped aside. She walked past him in a cloud of floral perfume. The scent was pleasant enough, and he'd smelled it enough times, but for the first time his nose picked up a synthetic after-note.

He knew it was unfair, but he couldn't help comparing it to the orange-blossom-infused scent Brandi wore. Fresh and down-to-earth, just like the woman.

Adam watched his ex take in the place he'd grown to think of as home. While he found it quiet and enjoyed the convenience of the walkable community's nearby town center, it was a long way from the second-floor wing he used to occupy in the palatial Ellison mansion.

"I haven't had a lot of time to dedicate to interior design, so you have a choice of a seat here in the dining room or in the kitchen."

"Anywhere is fine."

"Can I get you anything?"

Jade tossed her bone-straight, precision-cut weave over her shoulder. "Water, please."

She walked with him to the kitchen where he handed her a bottle of water from the fridge. She was staring at the two chocolate cakes on the kitchen island.

"So you actually made these?" she asked incredulously. "Yourself?"

Adam nodded.

"They're magnificent," she said. "I had no idea… When did you learn to do something like this?"

"My grandfather taught me when I was a boy."

"I never knew."

"There are a lot of things we didn't know about each other." He sat down on one of the swivel stools facing the kitchen island. "You didn't stick around long enough to find out."

He was surprised to see an uncharacteristic look of contrition pass over her flawless brown face. "I know, and I wish I'd handled things differently, but you blindsided me with all the sudden changes," she said. "Also, there was Brooks Brand to consider."

"We broke up months ago, Jade. Why are you here?" he finally asked.

Unbuttoning her coat, she put her purse on the island's countertop and took the seat next to him.

"These months without you have been harder than I expected," she said. "I've missed you. I've missed us."

Adam took a good look at the woman he'd come close to marrying. Kyle and his Uncle Jonathan were right. Jade was indeed very attractive in an airbrushed-magazine-cover-girl kind of way.

"In retrospect, I know I should have been more patient," she continued. "You'd suffered a tremendous loss. I should have been more understanding."

His initial anger at her turning her back on him along with everyone else had faded. Time had given him perspective, and he now knew she had done the right thing.

Adam shrugged. "You were right to break it off."

She reached out and covered his hand with hers. "Then why do I regret it so much?"

He gently removed her hand, sending the silent signal that it was over. "I'll always care about you, Jade."

"I care for you, too, very much. It wasn't just business for me, I really do love you."

Unmoved by her admission, Adam shook his head. "You love what we represented. You loved being half of a power couple."

"Of course I did. So did you," she said.

"I'm no longer willing to let business dictate my personal life, and you shouldn't, either. Don't sell yourself short, Jade. You're more important than Brooks Brand."

Jade rose from her chair and slung her purse over her shoulder. "If that's what you believe, then you're naive," she said. "Together we would have been worth billions."

"It's not going to happen for us. You should move on."

"I already have," she said, but she didn't sound happy about it.

"Then why come here?"

"I wanted to see if there was any way to salvage my old life, the one with you, before I officially moved on with my new one."

"Good luck with your new life, Jade." He stood, leaned over and kissed her lightly on the cheek. "I wish you all the best."

Brandi watched the scowl on her mother's face deepen as she crossed her arms over her chest and tapped her foot.

The staccato beat of her shoe echoed on the living room's hardwood floors.

"I know what I saw," Jolene Collins said. "They were kissing, Brandi. Kissing! Why do you think I came right back in here to tell you?"

Brandi sat on her sofa wrapped in her robe. She'd shed her workout clothes and was about to jump in the shower when her mother had come charging back into the condo.

"Mom, I'm sure there's a reasonable explanation," Brandi said aloud, silently hoping like hell it was true.

Her mother, however, wouldn't be mollified. "I've seen this man exactly twice. The first time you're plastered all over him, and less than a half hour later, he's in a lip-lock with another woman."

It was all Brandi could do not to cover her ears and scream at her mother to shut up. She didn't want to hear this. She didn't want to consider that the man, who'd only last night made her feel like the most beautiful and cherished woman in the world, was at this very moment with someone else.

"The woman was breathtaking. She looked like a model or actress," Jolene said.

Brandi pulled the belt of her robe tighter as if the action would deflect the sting of her mother's words. But like a boxer looking for a win, her mother picked up on her vulnerability and landed a knockout blow.

"I told you he looked like a man who could have any woman he wanted. Didn't I warn you he was out of your league?" Her mother ranted as she paced the floor.

Brandi tried to swallow the lump of hurt and anger rising in her throat as she'd done so many times before. Only this time, it wouldn't go down.

"How could you, Mom?" Brandi's voice trembled with unspoken pain.

"Me? What are you talking about?" Her mother huffed. "It's your friend from next door you should be questioning, not me."

"No, Mom." Brandi shook her head slowly. "Even if everything you say is true, Adam couldn't possibly hurt me as much as you have over the years."

Her mother stopped midpace. "I've done no such thing."

"Just stop it, Mom." Brandi held up a silencing hand. "All you've done since Dad died is pick me apart with your constant criticism."

Brandi felt years of tension ebb away as she finally let go of the words she'd been holding back so long. "Nothing I do seems to please you, and I'll tell you, Mom, I'm sick and damned tired of trying."

"Brandi Collins. How dare you curse me!"

"No, how dare *you,* Mom. How dare you nitpick me about my weight. How dare you insult me at every turn. And how dare you try to make me feel like nothing I ever do is good enough."

"What you call nitpicking is what I consider helping," her mother shot back. "You'd be so much prettier if you dropped those extra pounds."

"Oh, my God, there you go again."

"What? Are you so thin-skinned, you can't handle a bit of constructive criticism?"

"It's not constructive. It's mean and it's hurtful, and I don't know how much more of it I can take."

Her mother fisted her hands on her hips, and her face turned three shades of red before settling on an angriest.

"Don't you try making me out to be the bad guy here," she said through gritted teeth. "There's absolutely nothing wrong with a parent having high expectations for her children. It's not wrong for me to want my girls to look and be their very best. I'm not *mean* because I pushed you and your sister to get your college degrees in solid professions and want you to marry men of the same professional caliber."

Brandi felt like she was beating her head against a brick wall. What had happened to turn the sweet, nurturing mother of her childhood into this hard, unrelenting woman?

"You shoved me into a career I never wanted."

"I did what was best for you—my job as a parent," Jolene said. "I wanted you and Erin to do better than me and your father. To have better. To be better."

"Don't bring Daddy into this. All he ever wanted was for us to be happy," Brandi said.

"Happiness doesn't put food on the table."

"What are you talking about? We never went hungry."

"Thanks to me," her mother snapped.

"Oh, come on. Daddy was an excellent provider, who left you well taken care of when he died."

"All he left me was bills and you girls," Jolene muttered.

"What did you say?"

Her mother put her hand over her mouth. "Nothing," she said. "Look, I only came back to warn you about that guy next door. Not to open this can of worms."

Brandi watched her mother turn to go, but walked past her and blocked the door. "No, Mom. I want to know what you were talking about," she said.

"It was a long time ago, and there's no sense in dredging it up now."

"When Dad died I remember you telling me we'd be okay because he had investments and life insurance."

Her mother diverted her eyes. "Yes, that's what I told you."

"Was it the truth?"

Brandi watched Jolene's lips firm into a stubborn line.

"You might as well tell me, because you're not leaving until you do," she said, still blocking the door.

Their standoff lasted a few minutes before her mother relented and took a seat on the couch.

"Now tell me," Brandi said. "What really happened after Daddy died?"

Brandi didn't want to put herself or her mother through the pain of those dark days, but somehow she knew the reasons for her mother's change were tied to them.

Sitting on the sofa with her hands clasped in her lap, the domineering Collins matriarch suddenly looked smaller, older and very fragile.

"There were no investments or insurance," she finally whispered. "Just bills."

"But you said…"

Her mother shrugged her small shoulders. "Your father worked construction. It was good money, but the work was seasonal. My little secretarial paycheck had to tide us over for the rest of the year," she said. "There wasn't money for investments. He was a young man. We didn't think about life insurance."

"Why didn't you tell me?" Brandi asked.

"You adored your father. He was your larger-than-life hero. Memories of him were all you had left, and I didn't want anything to tarnish them."

"So you let me believe he'd taken care of us."

Jolene nodded. "I know you, Brandi. If you'd known you would have skipped college and went to work to help out."

"Of course I would have."

"I didn't want you to end up working a grunt job like me and your father. I wanted you to have your education."

Stunned, Brandi plopped down on the sofa next to her mother. "But food, clothing, not to mention keeping up the mortgage, paying for my college, opening your business. How did you do all of that?"

"By working day and night until I was ready to drop, then working some more."

Brandi reached across the sofa and took her mother's hand. Suddenly, she felt small and petty for the resentment she'd felt toward her over reimbursing her for the wedding. She'd owed her that much and more.

"Mom," she began.

"I know what you want from me, Brandi, but I'm not that person anymore. Struggle changes people," she said. "I am who I am."

No matter how hard she wished for her mother to be the way she used to be, it would probably never happen, Brandi realized sadly.

Somehow she'd have to find a common ground to build a relationship with the woman her mother was now.

Chapter 13

After Jade's exit, Adam went directly to Brandi's. She was due at his place to sample the cakes, but after what her mom had witnessed, and undoubtedly told her, he wasn't sure she'd show.

Brandi opened the door wrapped in the purple flannel robe she'd worn the night they'd met. He took one look at her red-rimmed eyes and knew her mother had given her a skewed version of events.

He walked through the door and followed her through to her living room, where she sat down in the armchair. A crumpled tissue was on the end table next to it.

"Is it true?" she asked, without preamble.

"Yes. It's true my ex-fiancée came to visit, and yes, she did kiss me. However…" He paused and held up his hands, wanting to make sure she heard the entire story. "I had no idea she was coming over. Until today, I haven't seen or heard from Jade in months."

Seeing Brandi upset summoned his protective instincts and made him annoyed her mother had stirred up a mess over what was essentially nothing. However, if he were completely honest with himself he couldn't fault the woman for looking out for her daughter.

"Look, I've just had an emotional scene with my mother, and I'm not in the mood for any more drama today," she said. "Besides, you're a free agent. One night in bed doesn't give me the right to question you."

Adam dropped his chin to his chest. *How did they get from those giddy moments in the corridor earlier to here?* he asked himself. One thing he knew for sure was he didn't want to leave things like this. He'd worked too hard to get close to her to let doubts come between them.

"I'm sorry about whatever went on with your mother. Do you want to talk about it?"

She shook her head.

"Well, I need to talk. You don't have to say anything, but please hear me out."

He felt a wave of relief at the brief incline of her head.

"For one thing, I don't think of last night as simply a night in bed. I consider it the beginning of something very special, *and exclusive.*"

Adam gave her a moment to absorb his words. He needed her to believe she was the only woman he wanted.

"Jade kissed me at the exact same moment your mother walked into the corridor," he continued. "What your mother didn't see was me peeling Jade off me. Nor did she notice I wasn't returning the kiss."

Brandi's eyes remained downcast, her attention focused on the tissue she was shredding in her hands. "My mom also mentioned she's very beautiful. I believe breathtaking was the word she used."

"She is," Adam agreed, "on the outside."

"I see." Her eyes were still downcast.

"I don't think you do. Superficial beauty isn't good enough for me anymore."

"It was enough for you to ask her to marry you."

Adam ran a hand over his head. His short engagement to Jade seemed like a lifetime ago. His life and goals had done a complete turnaround since they were together.

"I admit, at the time, I thought she was what I wanted," he said. Her and Brooks Brand, he thought, but was too embarrassed to divulge it to Brandi.

Still, he needed to give her some kind of explanation.

"Long story made less long, Jade wanted Adam the prominent businessman, not Adam the unemployed, wannabe pastry chef."

"Has she changed her mind?"

Adam shook his head. "No, she wanted to know if I'd changed mine. For the record, I haven't. I count leaving my old job and Jade breaking it off with me as the second and third best things to happen to me in a long time."

"And the first?"

"Meeting you."

Finally, a hint of a smile tugged at her mouth, and she threw up her hand in a dismissive wave. "You're smoother than your chocolate ganache."

Adam rose from the sofa. He walked over to the chair she was sitting on, took her hand and pulled her to her feet. "You believe me, don't you?"

She averted her gaze and chewed at her bottom lip. "I want to…"

Adam lifted her chin with the tip of his forefinger until her eyes met his. "You can trust me, Brandi."

His hopes dipped as she slowly shook her head. "It's just… I've been burned, and yes, I know you're not him.

I'm not trying to make you pay for what another man did, but at the same time…"

"I know you have baggage, and it makes it harder for you to take what I say at face value," he said. "Also, we haven't known each other very long."

"Then you understand?"

"I do. Trust isn't easy for you." He dropped his finger from her chin, wrapped his arms around her and pulled her into a tight hug. She rested her head on his shoulder, and he held her close, so close he could feel the gentle thump of her heartbeat through her robe.

Finally, he loosened his embrace, but he wasn't ready to let go. Nor was he willing to give up on her. Or let her give up on them.

"I consider your heart precious cargo. I'll always do my best to protect it, not break it."

She brushed her knuckles across his cheek. "That has to be the absolute sweetest thing anyone has ever said to me."

"I mean it." Adam closed his eyes briefly and blew out a breath, summoning the mental toughness to push aside his desire and keep his personal pledge to do right by this woman. "That's why I think it would be best if we put the intimate aspect of our relationship on hiatus."

"So we go back to being simply neighbors?" Brandi asked.

"No, we don't go back. We move forward as in going out on genuine dates, you know, dinner, the movies, dancing, an occasional concert. It'll give you time to learn that you trust me implicitly," he said. "Besides, after last night, we'll never be simply neighbors."

Brandi nodded mutely.

"Now get dressed." He dropped a kiss on top of her head and released her. "You have cakes to taste."

Chapter 14

"What about this one?"

Brandi glanced up from the rack of dresses to the one Lynn held up. She rolled her eyes skyward at the clingy, silver-metallic material covered in a faux-snakeskin pattern.

"You're supposed to be helping me pick out a dress, not a Halloween costume," she snapped.

She and her friend had come to the upscale Green Hills consignment shop after school the following Monday to hunt down a dress for Brandi's date with Adam that evening. He was taking her to dinner to celebrate the fact they'd perfected his entries for the competition this upcoming weekend.

Thanks to the weeks of torture sessions with Heather, Brandi was down a full dress size, leaving her with a closet full of baggy clothes.

"Geez, you're crabby these days," Lynn said. "How

long has it been again since you had your special *tasting* at your neighbor's?"

"Almost two weeks," Brandi grumbled. She'd spent the majority of the time kicking herself for, in her silence, agreeing to Adam's proposal to put the brakes on sex. It had seemed like a good idea at the time, and the best way for her to absolve herself of the trust issues lingering from the whole Wesley debacle.

Now she wasn't so sure.

Spending time with him every evening, whether going to dinner and a movie or giving input on his latest chocolate creation, was leaving her increasingly frustrated.

One more chaste kiss good-night, and she was going to drag him into her bedroom and slam the door behind them.

Lynn pulled another dress from the rack she was searching through. This one was cherry red with a short skirt and a deep, one-shoulder neckline Brandi hadn't seen the likes of since a rerun of the movie *Flashdance* on late-night television.

"This is cute." Her friend turned the dress around on the hanger to give her a view of the back.

"Yeah, for a hooker attending the Player's Ball."

Lynn returned the dress to the rack and planted her hands on her hips. "I wish you'd let him give you a tune-up, because you're becoming grouchier by the day."

Brandi turned away from the rack of staid, black dresses she'd been thumbing through and blew out a sigh.

"I'm sorry, Lynn," she said. "I don't understand it. Between Wesley and I deciding to abstain from sex after we got engaged to make our honeymoon more special and the six months after our breakup, I went over a year without it. No problem." She threw up her hands. "I sleep with Adam one time, now two weeks without it has turned me into a royal bitch."

Lynn shrugged and went back to searching the dress rack. "Maybe with Wesley there wasn't so much to miss."

Brandi smirked despite herself. Her friend made a good point.

At the time, Brandi had thought what she and her ex had was perfectly fine. Okay, so it wasn't earthquake or sky-rocket worthy, but until Adam she'd thought that was all just a bunch of bull *Cosmo* used to sell magazines to gullible single women.

"Imagine eating a single bite of the most fabulous dessert ever, and then it's abruptly snatched away," Brandi said glumly. "Then you'll have an inkling of how I feel right now."

"Get your nose out of those grandma dresses and into something like this," her friend held up a gold spandex dress with the back cut down to butt-crack level, "and Adam won't be able to keep his hands to himself."

"C'mon, Lynn, I can't wear that. He managed to get us a table at Ambience."

"Then the man must be totally smitten," her friend said. "I tried calling for reservations after the big write-up about them in the *Tennessean,* and they were booked solid. The snooty guy who answered the phone told me to try again in a few months."

"So please help me find an appropriate dress. My old ones are baggy, and I don't have time to take them in."

Brandi's phone rang and she fished it from the bottom of her tartan-plaid bag. Her mother's number flashed across the small screen.

Lynn peeked at the phone face and shook her head hard. "Don't answer it," she whispered as if she feared the caller would hear.

Brandi's mother had been busy nailing down last-minute wedding details, and they'd only seen each other once since they'd talked that day at her condo. Brandi had taken her mom out for lunch at her favorite Chinese restaurant last week, where to her credit, Jolene only mentioned her weight twice.

"Hi, Mom," Brandi said into the phone, ignoring Lynn's scowl.

Brandi listened as her mother launched into a tirade over Erin's whereabouts.

"Yes, I did know Erin was taking off to Atlantic City for a bachelorette bash with her girlfriends," Brandi answered.

Lynn held up another dress, this one a slinky cowl-neck. Only the cowl came down to the navel.

Brandi scrunched up her nose.

"I didn't try to stop her, Mom. No, she didn't invite me to come along." She and Erin were as close as they could be considering their twelve-year age difference. Brandi wasn't offended her sister hadn't asked her to join them.

She was trying to abide by her mother's and Erin's wishes for her to mind her own business. If her baby sister wanted to enjoy her last days as a single woman partying with her friends instead of attending a traditional bridal shower hosted by her mother and decade-older sister, so be it.

Her mother hit her with another barrage of questions.

"I'm sure she knows it's February and the wedding is next week."

Brandi held up an embroidered-lace black sheath for Lynn's perusal, and her friend held her nose in lieu of a reply.

"If you really need to get in touch with her, I'm sure Maurice has her hotel info and itinerary."

Apparently, he didn't.

"Well, I don't know what to tell you, Mom."

Actually, Brandi did know where Erin was staying, but

her sister had sworn her to secrecy. Besides, a few days away from her overbearing fiancé and their mother would be good for Erin.

"Sorry, can't do it tonight. I have a date," Brandi said. "Yes, it's with the gigolo from next door."

"Gigolo?" Lynn asked, after Brandi had ended the call.

"She's convinced he's only seeing me for my money."

"What money?" Lynn asked, still holding her sides from laughing.

"Didn't you know?" Brandi snorted. "I'm really a secret millionaire."

Lynn pulled a scarlet cross-front dress from the rack and held it out to her. Brandi picked up the hem and tried to imagine herself in the formfitting wrap dress with shirred skirt and leg-revealing slit.

"Pretty, but the color is a bit daring, don't you think?"

"Try it on, Miz Moneybags."

Brandi checked the price tag before taking the dress and heading toward the dressing room. "Speaking of moneybags, Adam's been taking me out quite a lot, and I feel guilty about him always paying. After all, I'm the one with the job."

"Has he complained?" Lynn stood outside the dressing-room door as Brandi changed.

"Just the opposite, he insists. I know his condo's paid off. Still, he's living off his savings."

"He knows best what he can afford, but if you're concerned then grab the check before he does."

Brandi stepped outside the dressing-room door to give Lynn a look at the dress.

"Wow!" Lynn's eyes widened. "You're looking hot."

Brandi ventured a look in the mirror, and her reflection caught her by surprise. She did look kind of hot.

"How many pounds have you lost again?" her friend asked.

"Only nine, but I've shaved off a lot of inches," Brandi said. "Heather says I've built muscle, and it takes up less room than fat."

Brandi did another turn in the mirror.

"All I'm saying is if you wear that dress tonight, you may not be so grumpy tomorrow morning." Lynn winked.

Twenty minutes later, the two were walking out of the store, Brandi carrying a bag with the red dress plus the pair of shoes she'd found to wear with it.

"Do you mind walking around the corner with me?" Brandi asked.

"Not at all. James doesn't get off his shift until tomorrow afternoon, so I don't have to make dinner," she said. "You want to check out the spot for Arm Candy?"

Brandi nodded. She liked walking past *her* store and imagining how she'd set up business there. Now that the children's clothing store had pulled up stakes, it was that much closer to being hers.

If only one of the microloans she applied for would come through soon, she thought. So far she only heard from one lender with a rejection.

They rounded the corner and as the store came into view, Brandi stopped in her tracks. The "FOR LEASE" sign was gone, replaced with a "COMING SOON" banner for a gourmet dog-biscuit bakery.

"We don't have to do this tonight," Adam said. "I can make a U-turn, call for pizza and have us home by the time the delivery guy arrives."

He caught Brandi's brief headshake in his peripheral vision as he steered the SUV off the interstate onto the narrow downtown streets leading to the restaurant.

She was putting up a good front, but Adam knew seeing the retail space she'd had her heart set on for her handbag boutique already leased had been a tremendous letdown.

"I hope you're not trying to weasel out of taking me to the hottest restaurant in town," she said. "Not after I bought a new dress and everything."

"And a knockout dress it is." He reached over the SUV's console and pulled back the flap of her coat. "It's a good thing you're wearing a coat, otherwise I might have accidently wrapped the car around a tree stealing glances at those legs of yours."

Brandi batted his hand away. "Keep your eyes on the road. I've looked forward to this meal ever since you told me you'd snagged reservations," she said. "How did you manage it, anyway?"

Adam shrugged. "In my old life, I brought business associates to Ambience for meals quite frequently."

Omar, the maître d' and also the co-owner of the popular restaurant, welcomed them the minute they walked through the door. "It's been a while. It's good to have you dining with us again."

He gave Adam's hand an enthusiastic shake before taking their coats.

"Glad to be back," Adam said. He turned his attention to Brandi. "Omar, I'd like you to meet my date, Brandi Collins."

Omar dipped his head. "Always nice to meet a beautiful woman."

Adam caught the hint of a blush flush Brandi's cheeks as she thanked him for the compliment.

"So, how've you been, Omar?"

"Business is great, so I'm great," the maître d' said. "I saved one of our best tables just for you and the lovely Miss Collins."

Adam placed a possessive hand on Brandi's back as Omar led them through the urbane restaurant. She was his, and he wanted the male eyes glued to the woman in the stunning red dress to know it. His date not only dazzled against the restaurant's understated decor, she made the other female diners, dressed in their cookie-cutter uniforms of boring black, look like attendees at an undertaker's convention.

"So far, the restaurant certainly lives up to its name." Brandi glanced around after Omar seated them at a corner table with plush microsuede banquettes on each side. It gave them privacy, but at the same time offered a view of the entire restaurant. "Thanks for the invite."

"It was the least I could do after all your help with my competition entries."

She shrugged. "All I did was eat a little chocolate. There isn't a woman alive who wouldn't have killed to be in my shoes."

Adam saw the sommelier armed with the wine list and waved him off. Instead, he ordered soft drinks from the waiter who'd brought their menus.

"You could have enjoyed a glass of wine," Brandi said. "I wouldn't have minded."

"The only thing I want to enjoy is your company."

Brandi's eyes narrowed as she opened her menu. "You're quite the flatterer this evening. If I didn't know better I'd think you were leading up to something."

"Then your instincts are right on target," Adam admitted.

Fortunately, their waiter returned to take their orders before she started asking questions.

"You're the regular here, what do you recommend?" she asked.

"Everything here is good. I'm partial to the scallops, but both the lamb and steak are quite good."

An hour later, they'd devoured salads, an appetizer of calamari tossed in cherry tomatoes and garlic butter, and plates of perfectly seared jumbo sea scallops accompanied by roasted asparagus and mashed-coconut, red-curry sweet potatoes.

And then faced a frowning Omar who had returned to their table.

"I just heard you two aren't having dessert," he said. "Surely you aren't going to pass on our special toasted lemon pound cake."

Adam checked with Brandi. "I wish I could, but I'm stuffed," she answered.

"Then I insist you at least have an after-dinner drink."

"They do make a marvelous cappuccino." Adam looked across the table at his date, who nodded her approval.

Once Omar was out of earshot, Brandi leveled him with a stare. "Now that we've eaten and made small talk, are you going to tell me what you've been buttering me up for?"

Adam took a deep breath and slowly released it. "As you know, the competition is this weekend."

"When are you leaving?"

"We," he corrected. "I'd like you to come with me."

"I'd love to!" Her face lit up. "Did you think you'd actually have to persuade me?"

Adam took a sip of the cappuccino the waiter dropped off at their table and relaxed for the first time since the meal began. "You'd mentioned taking a week off work, but I wasn't sure with it being the weekend before your sister's wedding. I know you have a lot to do," he said. "But I'm very happy you've agreed to come. I consider you my good-luck charm. No way I can win this thing without you there."

"Your chances of winning are excellent whether I'm there or not." She reached across the table for his hand. "But I'd love to come cheer you on."

"We won't have a lot of time, but we should be able to squeeze in a few of the sites Paris has to offer."

"Paris?" Brandi sputtered over her sip of cappuccino. "I thought the competition was in Montreal."

A feeling of dread began to creep over Adam, replacing his short-lived elation. "No, the North American competition was in Montreal, the international final is in Paris."

"Please tell me you mean Paris, Tennessee, or Kentucky? Or maybe Texas?"

He shook his head slowly. "France."

Brandi pulled her hand back from his. "I'm sorry, Adam. I can't," she said. "It wouldn't be right for me to run off to Europe this close to Erin's wedding."

He couldn't hide his disappointment. "Yeah, that's what I'd thought."

Brandi sighed and her face went all dreamy. "It's too bad because I've always wanted to see Paris," she said. "And it would have been even more wonderful seeing it with you."

"What if we could be there and back *before* the wedding?"

Adam knew it was selfish as hell of him to press her, but he really had come to think of her as his good-luck charm. He wanted her there. She wanted to be there.

"God, you don't know how much I want to say yes," she said. "But it's not just the wedding, there's the rehearsal dinner the night before and my mother or Erin might need me."

"Isn't your sister still in Atlantic City?"

Brandi nodded. "Which means she'll be rushed and frazzled when she gets home and will need me that much more."

It wasn't for him to say, but it seemed to him if the bride wasn't even in town, Brandi should be able to slip away for the weekend.

"You said yourself that your mother is an organizational dynamo who had every single detail of the wedding under control." Adam continued to build his case. "It's just for the weekend."

"But Europe is an ocean away."

"I'll have you back in Nashville Monday evening, in plenty of time for Tuesday night's rehearsal dinner."

Brandi chewed at her bottom lip, and he could tell she was on the brink of reconsidering. "But won't you be busy the day before the competition? I'd only be in the way."

Deciding to use his negotiating skills to their best effect, he used a different carrot. "Actually, it would give you time to explore the fabric district."

Brandi's eyes widened and she straightened in her chair. "Fabric district?"

"Wholesale fabric district. It's near the Sacré-Coeur," he said. "But I'm sure the last thing you want to do is spend hours pawing through a bunch of fabric, threads and buttons for Arm Candy."

"Enough. I give up. I'll go." Brandi held up her hands in mock surrender. "Oh, but there is something I'd like you to do for me."

"Name it."

"Would you be my date for Erin's wedding?"

"I'd love to," he said. "Now here's another question for you. Can you be packed and ready for Paris by Thursday?"

She nodded. "Packed? All I need is a big empty suitcase to bring home all my new French fabric booty."

Noticing they were done with the after-dinner coffees, the waiter stopped at the table. "Will there be anything else?"

"No, we're ready for the check," Adam said.

The waiter went to put the leather holder containing the bill on the table, and Brandi snatched it up quickly. "I'll take that," she said.

"Brandi, I invited you. The meal is on me."

As if she hadn't heard a word he'd said, she placed her credit card in the holder and handed it back to the waiter.

"It's always your treat. Now it's my turn."

"I pay because that's what a gentleman does on a date," Adam said firmly.

Brandi blew out an impatient breath. "Look, I'm not trying to embarrass you, but you don't have a job right now and I do."

"But I told you I have…"

"Yeah, I know, you have savings, but they can't last forever."

Maybe not forever, but certainly a lifetime or two, Adam thought.

"I'm paying," she said. "End of story."

Adam watched her sign the credit card receipt and return her card to her wallet. "Okay, you win this time," he said as they walked toward the front of the restaurant to collect their coats. "Thanks for dinner."

Adam heard Omar's slightly raised voice before they reached the maître d's stand.

"Your reservation was for two hours ago. You didn't call to say you'd be delayed, so your table is no longer available," Omar said firmly.

Adam momentarily wondered who would be arrogant enough to show up late to a hot ticket like Ambience. He didn't have to wait long for the answer.

"I don't think you realize who you're talking to. I'm…"

The voice was familiar enough that Adam didn't need to hear the name. He caught the man's surprised eye, just as he finished his sentence.

"…Zeke Holden, and my wife and I would like a table."

Wife?

Adam's head snapped up. He looked from Zeke to the woman standing next to him. *Jade?*

The three of them stared at each other openmouthed.

Meanwhile, the puzzle pieces quickly assembled themselves in Adam's head. Zeke's strange behavior of late. Jade's impromptu visit and her last-minute plea for a reconciliation before moving on with her new life.

"Congratulations." Adam broke the awkward silence.

Zeke ran a hand across his head. "Look, man, I didn't mean for you to find out about me and Jade like this. I was going to tell you, but everything happened so fast."

"So this was the mystery woman you assured me I didn't know?" Adam asked.

"Like I said, it all happened quickly. One minute, my dad and I were hammering out a business deal with Jade's father, and the next I was falling for his daughter," his friend said, unable to look him in the eye. "Business is business. Hope you're not mad. No hard feelings, right?"

The glint of Jade's diamond wedding set caught Adam's eye, and he could honestly say he wasn't angry. However, he was deeply disappointed.

Not in Jade, but in Zeke.

Adam didn't want Jade or her company and would have given Zeke his blessing. However, Zeke hadn't been man or friend enough to mention to him he was going after them.

"Again, congratulations," Adam said.

Omar passed their coats, and Adam helped Brandi with hers. "Let's go, sweetheart."

"Sweetheart?" Jade spoke for the first time. She eyed Brandi. "And you are?"

"Brandi Collins, meet my ex-fiancée, Jade Brooks, I mean Jade Holden and her new husband, Zeke," Adam said.

"I didn't realize you were seeing anyone." Jade's voice was a whisper.

"Well, I guess we're all full of surprises," Adam replied, but his gaze remained on his friend, who still wasn't able to look him in the eye.

"Again, congratulations," Adam said. "I wish you two the best."

Chapter 15

Brandi wasn't exactly sure what she'd witnessed back at the restaurant, but Adam seemed oddly calm for someone who'd just found out his ex-fiancée was married to his friend.

"Are you okay?" she ventured ten minutes into the drive back to their condos.

"Yeah, I am," he said.

"So that was your ex, huh?"

He nodded and thumbed the control on the steering until the smooth sounds of a vintage Jill Scott tune filled the SUV's cabin.

"Things seemed tense with you and her new husband," she said. "Just how close of a friend is he to you?"

He sighed before he spoke. "Up until tonight, I'd considered him a good friend."

"Ouch," Brandi said. "Do you think he really meant what he said about wanting to tell you?"

Adam shook his head. "Zeke's been avoiding me for weeks. I even drove out to his place to make sure he was okay. He could have told me then. Instead, he blew me off. Said he had a big date with someone I didn't know."

"Jade," Brandi concluded.

"Evidently," he said. "Don't get me wrong, I'm not still hung up on Jade. However, Zeke didn't know that. He didn't think enough of me or our friendship to be upfront."

"He doesn't sound like much of a friend to me."

Adam snorted. "My brother never trusted him, but Zeke and I have similar backgrounds. I thought I knew him."

"What about Jade?" Brandi couldn't help asking. The look of longing in the woman's eyes when she looked at Adam's was obvious. So was the contemptuous expression in those same eyes when Adam had briefly introduced them.

"Jade didn't betray me. I told her to move on."

"That's what her visit was about, wasn't it?" Brandi asked. "She wanted to give you first dibs on her before she married him."

"Pretty much."

"Do you regret turning her away?" Brandi asked.

Her mother's description of Jade had been no exaggeration. Adam's ex was flawless. No man turns away a woman that looked like her with no regrets, Brandi thought.

He spared her a glance before returning his eyes to the road. "Why do you find it so hard to believe I had practically thrown her out of my place to come running straight to you?"

"The woman is stunning," Brandi said.

"Hmm," Adam said.

"Don't you think so?"

"Honestly, I have no idea. I've never seen Jade sans her perfect weave, expertly applied makeup, fake nails and saline boobs." Adam steered the car onto the interstate. "On the other hand, I know what you look like ranting at me about chocolate at three in the morning, sweaty from a grueling workout or pushing through exhaustion for the sake of your business," he said. "I've seen your hair disheveled from me running my fingers through it, your lips swollen from my kisses and the expression of utter bliss on your face after I've made you come."

Brandi gripped the armrest to keep from melting into the Porsche's butter-soft leather seat.

"Those are the things I believe are beautiful." He reached across the console for her hand and brought it to his lips in the sweetest kiss she'd ever experienced. "Not only can they not be purchased, they're priceless."

Brandi looked through the passenger-side window and discreetly wiped a tear from her eye. His words had done more than touch her emotionally.

Deep down she knew.

She'd been guarding her heart against the man it already belonged to.

The sound of knocking roused Adam from a deep sleep.

He'd passed out in the living room chair again, the twenty-four-hour sports network on the television watching him. It had become routine since his night with Brandi.

One night together and his bed felt lonely without her.

It had taken more restraint than he thought he possessed to say good-night at her door with just a kiss, but the next time he made love to Brandi he wanted her to be free of the baggage from her last relationship. He'd wait as long as it took because he wanted more than her body—he wanted her heart.

The pounding at the door kicked up again. Adam

yawned and stretched the kinks out of his back. He squinted at his watch until the numbers came into focus.

"It had better be the fire department evacuating the building," he grumbled, because he couldn't think of another reason someone would be paying him a visit at five o'clock in the morning.

He looked through the peephole before yanking the door open.

"Aren't you usually in some woman's bed at this hour?" he asked.

"Just left," his brother quipped as he walked through the door. "What did you do, sleep in your clothes, bro?"

Adam glanced down at the suit pants and wrinkled dress shirt he hadn't bothered changing out of before he'd plopped down in front of the television last night. He followed his brother, who was apparently also wearing clothes from the night before, and found him rummaging through the kitchen cabinets.

"I'm starving." Kyle opened the refrigerator and surveyed the contents. "The problem with models is they don't eat, so they don't get up and make breakfast." He grabbed the orange juice and drank straight from the carton.

"Kyle," Adam snapped and his early-morning guest stopped gulping down juice and faced him. "No offense, but what in the hell do you want this early in the morning?"

Kyle's cocky demeanor vanished. He put the juice down, leaned back on the kitchen counter and folded his arms. He glanced down at the floor before looking up at him.

"I don't know how to say this, but…"

The look on his younger brother's face worried him. "You okay?"

"I wanted to tell you before you heard it somewhere else."

"Jade married Zeke," Adam finished for him.

His brother's jaw dropped. "How did you find out so quickly? When I saw them eating dinner at the country club, Jade said she'd eloped to Vegas with that arrogant prick and had only returned to Nashville yesterday evening."

"I saw them earlier trying to get a table at Ambience."

"How the hell did you get a table at Ambience? I've been trying to eat there for months."

Adam shrugged.

"Sorry you had to find out like that. That's why I came straight over, well, right after I left Ariel's," Kyle said.

"Ariel? What happened to Greta?" Adam teased.

"Who?" Kyle looked genuinely dumbfounded. "Anyway, what did they have to say for themselves?"

Adam yawned. "Zeke gave me some bad Lifetime movie spiel about wanting to tell me, but the time was never right."

"Please tell me you don't believe him. I'll bet he made his play for both her and Brooks Brand as soon as he'd heard you dropped out."

"You're probably right. In fact, you were right about Zeke being untrustworthy all along."

"I'll also bet Vegas was that sneaky bastard's idea, and he couldn't care less about Jade. Him and his father just wanted to get their greedy hands on Brooks Brand."

"Jade seemed to know what she was getting into," Adam said. "Still, I don't understand how Zeke convinced her to go for a quickie wedding. When we got engaged, she didn't want a wedding day, she wanted a weeklong celebration," he said. "Who knows? Maybe it's true love."

Kyle already appeared to have lost interest in the topic.

"Hey, I apologize for how that whole blowup went down last time I was here. I was out of line."

Adam nodded. "I could have handled things better myself."

"For someone whose ex just hooked up with his best friend, you don't seem too broken up," Kyle said. "You really meant it when you said you two were over. I'd thought your breakup and this chocolate thing you're pursuing were just part of a midlife crisis."

Adam moved past his brother and reached for the bag of coffee beans. It didn't look like Kyle was going anywhere soon, so he might as well get the coffee started.

"I don't know if thirty-five qualifies as midlife, but I'm serious about this competition. In fact, I'm headed to Paris this weekend for the final judging."

"Well, that throws a kink into my plans. I was going to take Ariel down to Miami, but if you're going to be hogging the jet all weekend…"

"I'm flying commercial," Adam said over the sound of the coffee grinder.

"Commercial." Kyle wrinkled his nose like he'd smelled something bad. "Don't you think you're taking this whole vow of poverty or whatever you're calling it too far?"

"I painted myself into a corner and don't have much of a choice." Adam switched on the coffeemaker and pulled two mugs from the cabinet. "I'm seeing someone, and I've asked her to accompany me to Paris for the competition."

"So?"

"She has no idea about my background. To her, I'm just an unemployed wannabe pastry chef. So I can't suddenly drive up to a private plane."

"You didn't tell her? Man, that's the first thing I tell a woman I want to impress."

Adam shook his head. "I kept it quiet, and it's not like she could connect any dots. You pick up any of our paper products, cleansers, detergents and they're all different companies under the Ellison Industries umbrella," he said. "When a customer picks up a jug of Tide at the grocery store, they're thinking Tide not Proctor and Gamble. And years ago, when Sara Lee owned Coach, I don't think many women associated pound cake with their leather purses."

"Who's the woman you're taking to Paris? Do I know her?"

"Yes, you've met her, nosy. She was at the door the day you stormed out."

"Oh, your neighbor. We crossed paths in the hallway this morning before I knocked on your door. She was dressed in workout clothes." Kyle drained the juice carton and stuck it back in the fridge. "She cleans up good. Looked way better than she did the first time I saw her."

Adam laughed at the thought about Brandi dressing down in the vintage velour track suit. He relayed the story to his brother as he filled the mugs with coffee.

"Well, it worked for me," Kyle said. "I was completely turned off."

"Good, playa. I don't need you sniffing around my woman," Adam joked.

"If you two are so tight, how come she wasn't leaving from your place this morning?"

Adam took a sip from his mug. "It's a long story, but once this competition is behind me and we get back from Paris, I plan to fill her in on my background and then do everything in my power to make Brandi Collins my wife."

Kyle shook his head and held up his mug in mock salute. "Damn, another dead soldier."

Chapter 16

Three days later, Brandi pressed her face to the glass of the chauffeured car's window and marveled at her first glimpses of Paris.

Paris. She bit back a girlish squeal of excitement.

Even as Adam pointed out the Eiffel Tower, the Arc de Triomphe and other iconic sites on the impromptu tour he'd directed the driver to take them on en route to the hotel, Brandi still could hardly believe she was in the City of Lights.

"Any regrets about leaving Nashville?" Adam asked.

"Not one." She kissed him and snuggled into his embrace in the backseat of the luxury car. This ranked highly among the best moments of her life, and she wanted to savor it.

"I promise to bring you back in the spring when it's not so cold and gray," he said. "It's beautiful here when everything is in bloom."

Brandi shook her head. "I don't think it can be any more perfect than it is right now."

A light coating of snow covered the ground when their plane had arrived at Charles de Gaulle airport. The butter-soft leather seats and delicious meal aboard the first-class transatlantic flight had spoiled her. She'd think of it every time she sat packed like a sardine aboard her usual discount airline munching a complimentary pack of stale peanuts.

They walked inside the lobby of their hotel located in the first arrondissement, and Brandi's mouth fell open at the splendor of the ornate, old-world decor. She smoothed a hand over a marble statuette before sinking into one of the plush, red-velvet armchairs and surveying the room's intricate woodwork and gilded crystal chandeliers.

After Adam checked in, a bellman led them upstairs to a luxurious suite that managed to maintain the nineteenth-century, Belle Époque charm of the lobby without sacrificing modern-day luxury.

The bellman wasn't out of the room a second when Adam pulled her into his arms. His mouth took possession of hers, and Brandi's fingers clung to his broad shoulders as his tongue teased and tantalized, sending ripples of delight through her.

"Do you know how hard it was to sleep in the seat next to you all night on that plane and keep my hands to myself?" he asked when they finally came up for air.

She pressed herself against him. "No, but I can feel how hard it is."

He released her and dropped a kiss to her forehead. "First, you'd better take a nap before jet lag kicks in," he said and she yawned. "If it hasn't already."

"But I want to see…" Another yawn short-circuited her protest. "Okay, but only for a few minutes."

Two and a half hours later, she awoke to find Adam stretched out beside her on top of the covers. He was on his side, smiling down at her with his head resting on the palm of his hand.

"Have I been dreaming or am I really in Paris?"

"We're really here," he confirmed.

She threw her arms over her head in a long, catlike stretch. "You smell good."

"I've already showered and changed."

She sat up abruptly and scooted toward the edge of the bed.

Adam pulled her back. "Hey, where are you off to so fast?"

"I can't sleep and stink through my first day in France." She kissed him on the mouth and scampered off to freshen up.

She emerged from the bathroom showered and dressed in a leopard-print pullover sweater paired with brown wool pants and leather ankle boots. The light in Adam's eyes when he saw her made her glad she'd taken extra care with her hair and makeup.

"Vous êtes trés belle."

"I know just enough French to know you said something very sweet." And it made her want to drag him right back on that king-size bed. "Thank you."

"De rien, Mademoiselle." He held out his hand to her. "Now come here, I want to show you something."

Adam opened the room's glass doors and led her onto the snow-covered balcony. The icy February wind sliced through her wool sweater and he came up behind her, staving it off with his embrace.

Keeping one arm wrapped protectively around her, he used the other to point out the highlights afforded by their panoramic view.

"There's the Jardin des Tuileries, which probably isn't much to look at in the height of winter. Over there you can see the Musée d'Orsay, and of course, straight on is the Eiffel Tower."

It was a gray, cold day and snow lined the streets, but none of it detracted from the heady feeling of being in the world's most romantic city with a man she was absolutely crazy about.

Brandi shivered, and reluctantly allowed herself to be led back inside.

"Adam, I know we agreed to settle up after the trip, but I don't know how many installments it's going to take to reimburse you for my half…."

He silenced her with a shake of his head and touched a finger to her lips. "We'll figure it out when we get home. For now, let's simply enjoy, okay?"

"Okay," she reluctantly agreed.

"Besides, you just got notified two of your microloans were approved before we left, right?"

Brandi nodded.

"So once you find a new spot for Arm Candy, it won't be long before you'll be bringing me to Paris."

Brandi laughed. She was buoyed by the news those loans were approved, but she was still holding out hope for the one from Lina Todd. Not only was it larger than the other two put together, it came with Lina's expertise.

Adam held out her coat and she slipped her arms into it. "I know you're eager to get out and explore the city, but do you mind if we make a detour?"

"Your grandmother?"

Adam nodded. "I have something for her. Also, I'd love for her to meet you."

"Of course I don't mind."

After a light meal in the hotel's restaurant, they took a

ten-minute taxi ride to Adam's grandmother's apartment in the city's Le Marais district.

Holding a wrapped gift box under his arm, Adam punched the code into the keypad to unlock a large wooden door to a very old stone building and led them through a courtyard. Three flights of stairs later, he knocked on the apartment door.

A tall woman with skin the same dark chocolate shade as Adam's answered. She wore slim Levi's on her lithe frame, ballet flats and oversize white shirt. Fine lines etched her smiling face, and her hair was a riot of kinky, silver curls.

"Adam." She held Adam's face between her wrinkled hands and pressed a kiss to his cheek. "It's so good to see your face, *mon chou.*"

The bangle bracelets encircling her wrist clinked as she beckoned them both inside the surprisingly modern dwelling. Considering the aging stone exterior of the building and his grandmother's age, Brandi had jumped to the conclusion she'd be walking into a space cluttered with lace doilies, ancient furniture and decades of mementos.

She couldn't have been more wrong. The small apartment made the same first impression as its owner. It was stylish, elegant and filled with natural light.

"It's the same face you see nearly every day via Skype," Adam told his grandmother.

She shook her head. "Skype and that fancy tablet computer you gave me are good, but they aren't a substitute for being able to hug my grandson."

Brandi felt Adam entwine his fingers with hers and pull her to his side. "*Mémé,* I have someone I want to meet," he said. "Brandi Collins, meet my grandmother, Catherine Rousseau."

The stylish elderly woman greeted her with a kiss on

each cheek. "My grandson told me you've been helping him perfect his recipes," she said. "Do you think he's ready for the competition?"

Brandi looked up at Adam as she answered the elderly woman's question. "Yes, I do," she said honestly. "He's an extraordinary pastry chef." *And I believe in him with all my heart,* she added silently.

Catherine touched her grandson's cheek. "He may look like me, but he has his grandfather's passion for pastry and chocolate. We both always knew it was just a matter of time before he started to fulfill his true destiny."

The elderly woman excused herself and left the room for a moment. When she returned she held several worn, leather notebooks held together by a red ribbon out to Adam. "These are yours now."

Brandi watched Adam's face as he took the books and thumbed though pages yellow with age. "It's Grandpa's recipe notes," he said, his voice filled with reverence.

"I've been selfishly holding on to them because they so remind me of him," his grandmother said. "But I know, especially now, he would want you to have them."

"Thank you, *Mémé.*"

Brandi could feel the emotion in his voice.

"Oh, I nearly forgot. I have something for you, too." Adam handed his grandmother a box wrapped in silver paper.

Brandi had forgotten about the red, poppy-flower print bag he'd bought from her until his grandmother pulled it from the white tissue paper and gasped.

"What a beauty. I'm going to be the envy of every woman at the market." Her eyes narrowed and focused on Brandi. "You must have had something to do with this, because my grandson's presents are usually the latest electronic gadgets. My mobile phone's so fancy, I don't know how to answer it when it rings."

"Actually, *Mémé,* Brandi made the bag. She's a handbag designer."

Catherine ran a wrinkled hand over her new bag. "You're a very talented young lady. The handiwork is exquisite."

Brandi thanked the older woman. "I'm planning to scour the city's fabric district for new material tomorrow while Adam's doing his last-minute prep for the competition."

"Would you like some company?" Catherine asked.

"I'd love some."

Catherine looped her arm through Brandi's. "Also, it'll be good to have someone to sit with during the competition. I just knew I'd be a nervous wreck sitting there alone."

"Me, too." Brandi laughed and stole a glance at Adam. "What are you grinning about?"

"I'm just thinking about the competition," he said. "Now that I have my two favorite ladies cheering me on, I can't lose."

Chapter 17

The wee morning hours the day of the competition found Adam much as he'd been since they'd left his grandmother's apartment: his head bent over the hotel room's small secretaire studying his grandfather's faded handwriting in the tattered notebooks.

The volumes' ragged appearance belied their pricelessness. They represented his grandfather's fifty years in pastry. The secrets, techniques, triumphs and catastrophes were all meticulously detailed in the familiar scrawl.

Unfortunately, they were in French, which slowed the pace at which Adam could get through them. Still, at this moment, he could not feel any closer to his late grandfather if he were sitting beside him.

He felt a light touch on his shoulders and lifted his chin to see Brandi standing behind him.

"You stayed up all night reading, didn't you?" She stood

behind him and massaged his shoulder blades with her fingertips.

Adam rolled his shoulders, feeling the stiffness in them ebb away under her gentle touch.

"The competition starts in a few hours. Shouldn't you try to get some rest?"

"I want to get through as much of them as I can before the competition begins," he said. "I can't explain it. I just do."

He lifted her hand from his shoulder and tugged her around the chair until she was sitting on his lap. "Thank you for being so understanding. It wasn't my intention to bring you all the way to Paris to pawn you off on my grandmother," he said.

"Don't be silly," she said. "Catherine is a joy, and I enjoyed spending yesterday with her. She also has excellent taste and helped me find some sensational remnants in the fabric district yesterday. Not to mention, she translated so I didn't have to bumble around with my French phrase book."

"Still, you've been a good sport about it, and when this is over, I promise to make it up to you."

Brandi encircled her arms around his neck. "I plan to hold you to that."

"You should get your beauty sleep," he said. "It'll be daylight in a few hours."

She nodded and started to get off his lap, but he pulled her back to him and kissed her long and deep. Her soft curves and rounded bottom felt so good against him, he didn't want to let go.

Brandi broke the kiss and inclined her head toward the journals.

"I'll let you get back to them," she said.

This time he reluctantly let her go, but couldn't resist

watching the sexy sway of her hips as she walked away, reminding him of everything he was missing as she crawled back into bed.

By noon, the competition was in full swing, and the large auditorium was buzzing with the sounds of harried chefs clanging about their individual spaces and the murmured conversation of the audience looking down at them from their stadium seat perches.

Adam spied Brandi and his grandmother sitting together, but hadn't been able to do much more than nod in their direction.

The jury of international judges had already come around to his table to taste the triple chocolate creation he prepared as his first entry, but he hadn't been able to glean any hints from their stone faces.

Not that it mattered.

Poring over his grandfather's notes had given Adam a new perspective to the competition and what it truly meant. Before he was using it as the sole barometer to judge his worthiness as a pastry chef and give him credibility.

He had made it all about himself and his ego when it should instead have been about his food and how it made those who ate it feel.

His grandfather's notes reminded him of being a boy and watching the patisserie's customers catch their breath at the sight of the day's offerings in the glass display cases, and the moans of pleasure accompanying their first bite of his chocolate tarts.

Or, in Adam's case, how the scent of his own pastries had lured the woman of his dreams to his doorstep.

It was about food and people, not sculptures or weird, trendy flavors. Just rich, intense, powerful, magical chocolate desserts and the people who loved them.

So when he donned his pristine white chef jacket and pleated chef hat that morning, he'd decided to ditch the entry he'd stressed over for weeks in lieu of a classic opéra cake using his grandfather's old recipe.

Absolutely no one made the almond sponge cake soaked in coffee syrup and layered with coffee buttercream and chocolate ganache as well as his late grandfather.

Adam slid the parchment-lined jelly-roll pans filled with batter for the sponge base into the oven. While they baked, he went to work at the stove. Three burners were on as he began to prepare the coffee syrup and chocolate ganache filling.

Adam had never made the French cake before. So all he had to go on were his instincts, an old recipe on faded paper and memories of watching his grandfather prepare it countless times.

The timer buzzed and he checked the status of the sponge cakes. Their light brown color was just right so he pulled them from the oven and immediately turned them off the pan.

Adam cut the cooled sponge into rectangles to fit the square pastry rings in which he'd assemble the cakes. Placing a layer of sponge in the bottom of each of the rings, he used a pastry brush to apply a generous layer of coffee syrup.

Over the next hour, he carefully layered the sponges with smooth buttercream, chocolate ganache and coffee-syrup fillings.

Adam chilled the cakes before completing the final stage of spreading chocolate glaze over the top layers of buttercream, gingerly removing them from the pastry squares and trimming away the rough edges.

The final cakes had a half hour to chill in the fridge

before the announcer signaled it was time for the judges to make their rounds.

Adam stood by his table as the judges began tasting the three opéra cakes he'd prepared. As with the earlier judging, their expression remained impassive.

When all was said and done, Adam claimed second prize, losing out to a chocolate praline cake from a chef from Denmark.

"You've made me so proud today," his grandmother said afterward.

Brandi touched the silver medal hanging around his neck. "I hope you're not too disappointed," she said. "Catherine's right. You've made us two extremely proud women today."

Before he could answer her, one of the judges approached them. The silver-haired man leaned on his cane with one hand and extended the free one to Adam.

"Chef Ellison, I wanted to tell you personally how absolutely superb your opéra cake was today," he praised in French-accented English. "I haven't tasted cake so delicious since Chef Rousseau's old patisserie in Le Marais."

Emotion rose in Adam's throat at the compliment, and he simply nodded his thanks, not trusting himself to speak.

"I'm Chef Rousseau's widow, Catherine, and Adam here is our grandson," his grandmother interjected.

"Ah, Madame Rousseau, you're every bit as lovely as you were when I used to visit your bakery years ago."

The two began talking in French and soon, Adam and Brandi found themselves alone as the two left together to discuss old times over an early dinner.

Adam wrapped an arm around Brandi. "To answer your question, I'm not disappointed at all." He pulled her closer and captured her gaze with his. "How could I even think of being disappointed when I'm in Paris with the woman I love?"

Brandi's eyes widened. "Love?"

He nodded. "And because the scent of it brought you into my life, I've already won chocolate's grand prize."

"Oh, Adam, I love you, too," she said.

He kissed her again, the taste of her mouth even sweeter now that he knew her heart truly belonged to him.

Brandi broke the kiss. "Let's get out of here."

"We have the rest of the day free before our flight tomorrow. Where do you want me to take you first? The Eiffel Tower? The Louvre?

She shook her head. "Back to the hotel. We've got a bed to break in, Mr. Dark Chocolate."

The next morning, Brandi awoke but kept her eyes closed. She wasn't ready to leave this bed or Paris.

As Adam had shown her repeatedly last night, it truly was a city for lovers.

And he'd told her he loved her.

She reached out for him, but opened her eyes when she discovered his side of the bed was empty.

"You still playing possum?" He was wrapped in his robe in front of the balcony sipping coffee and watching the snow come down.

"I wish we didn't have to go back." She threw back the covers.

"Don't bother getting up," he said. "Your wish was granted an hour ago."

"What do you mean?" She joined him in front of the balcony's glass doors. Snow blinded what yesterday had been a scenic view.

"It's been snowing all night. Both Paris airports are

closed. So is London's Heathrow," he said. "Europe hasn't seen a blizzard like this in over a decade."

Brandi felt a split second of elation, and then it quickly crashed. "Erin's wedding," she gasped.

"I've done some checking. If it stops when the forecasters predict, and the airports reopen, I can still have you back hours before the wedding. However, more than likely you'll miss the rehearsal dinner."

Brandi heaved a sigh. "I'd better check in with Erin and Mom to let them know I'll be delayed."

The conversation with her mother went about as expected. Jolene Collins wasn't pleased her elder daughter would be missing the rehearsal dinner. In contrast, her conversation with Erin was a breeze. Her sister had only just arrived home from Atlantic City the day before and was grateful Brandi's delay had diverted their mom's attention from her.

After the calls Brandi returned to Adam's side to watch the snowfall.

Adam put down his coffee, came up behind and wrapped his arms around her. She leaned back into his embrace. Even in the near-whiteout conditions, she could make out the outline of the Eiffel Tower in the distance.

"I hope you aren't too disappointed. I know I promised to have you home in time for the wedding festivities. I'll get us back as soon as the weather lets up."

She turned around and kissed him. "How could I even think of being disappointed?" she asked. "I'm in love and in Paris."

Chapter 18

There were six voice-mail messages awaiting Brandi on her cell phone when their plane finally landed in Nashville the afternoon of the wedding.

She began listening to them as the plane taxied to the gate, the first three from her mother panicking over whether Brandi would indeed make it home in time.

So she fast-forwarded to the fourth.

Beep: Brandi Collins, this is Lina Todd. I just viewed your video, and I'm very interested in talking to you about Arm Candy. Please give me a call at your earliest convenience.

Stunned, Brandi's hand shook as she held the phone. "Oh, my God! You're not going to believe this. Lina Todd called me yesterday. Oh, my God!" Brandi threw her arms around Adam's neck and hugged him. "She wants me to call her."

The plane stopped at the gate. He unbuckled his seat

belt and then hers. "Well, let's get off this tin can so you can return her call."

"Okay, but let me listen to the last two messages first. Maybe she left a second one."

The next voice Brandi heard on her voice mail was her sister's and it sounded like she'd been crying.

Beep: Brandi, it's me. Maybe rushing this wedding isn't such a good idea. Maurice has to have his own way about everything, all the time. Do this, Erin. No, it's that way, Erin. I know what's best, Erin. I don't want to mess up all of the plans, but I can't... I don't know. Just call me when you get this message."

Brandi's finger trembled as she pressed the button to move on to the last message, which was from a second call Erin made a few hours after the first.

Beep: It's me, again. Forget my last message. It was just a little case of cold feet. I talked to Mom, and then Maurice and I had a real heart-to-heart. They made me realize how silly I was being. So forget about all the nonsense I was babbling on about earlier. Everything is okay now. I'll see you when you get home. Love you."

Brandi felt Adam's hand on her shoulder as they exited the plane. "Everything okay?" Adam asked.

Her call from Lina Todd practically forgotten, Brandi shook her head. "Not really. I need to talk to my sister. Now." She glanced at her watch. The evening ceremony didn't start for another four hours. Time enough for her to make sure Erin wanted this wedding and the husband that came along with it.

Adam pulled his keys from his pocket. He removed his door key from the ring and pressed the one to his Cayenne into her palm. "Take my car and go to your sister," he said.

"What about the baggage? And how will you get home?"

"Don't worry about me. I'll see to our bags and grab a cab."

Relief coursed through her. "Thank you," she said.

He bent his head and kissed her lightly on the mouth. "I love you," he said.

Even in her frazzled state, his words made her heart turn a cartwheel in her chest. "Love you, too."

A half hour later she was walking through her mother's front door.

"Well, it's about time," her mother greeted, hands on hips. "And who does the Porsche you pulled up in belong to?"

"The gigolo," Brandi said, her sister the priority. "Where's Erin?"

"She's in her room. Her girlfriends are helping her get…"

Brandi immediately strode toward her sister's bedroom. She stopped abruptly at the doorway. Her baby sister looked beautiful, and she hadn't even donned her gown yet.

Sitting at her old vanity dressed in a white, satin dressing gown, Erin's hair was pulled into a chignon anchored by a delicate red rose. Rubies adorned her ears and neck, and her makeup was soft down to the red stain applied to her lips.

"Brandi, you made it!"

"Of course I'm here." Brandi looked past Erin to her friends. "I really need to talk to you. Alone."

Erin turned to Ashley, Tiffany and Taylor. "Will you guys go out and see if my mom needs anything? And try to keep her from coming in here and driving me nuts."

After her sister's trio of best friends made a giggly exit, Brandi closed the door. She pulled up a chair beside Erin.

"How was Paris?" Erin asked. "I can't believe you actually ran off to Europe for the weekend. It certainly tops my Atlantic City jaunt. When I get back from my honeymoon I want to hear all about it."

Brandi reached over and took her sister's hands in hers. "I got your messages." She fixed her with a pointed look.

"Oh, those," Erin said. "I already told you, it was just a minor case of cold feet. Thank God Mom and Maurice talked me down. I'm okay now."

Erin may have sounded upset during the first call, but the words had rung true. It seemed to Brandi that her sister had finally had a moment of clarity. "Erin, you don't have to do this today. If you're having second thoughts we can postpone the wedding until you've had time to be sure this is what you really want."

Her sister pulled her hands from Brandi's and gave her a reassuring pat. "Of course I want to get married. All of my friends are either getting engaged or married."

"And you're all very young." Too young, Brandi thought.

"Well, I don't want to look up one day and I'm over thirty and still single like…" Erin caught herself. "I'm sorry, I didn't mean it like that."

"It's okay. I just want you to be certain and that you're doing it for the right reasons. After all the hubbub of the wedding is over, it'll be just you and Maurice. No receptions. No pretty dresses."

Erin nodded. "I'm sure."

"But do you love him, Erin?"

Erin gave her a dismissive wave. "Of course. Who wouldn't want to marry a doctor?"

The fact her sister hadn't actually answered her question wasn't lost on Brandi. Not sure if anything she'd said had gotten through to her sister, she gave her one last thing to think about.

"When you're repeating your vows today, take a really

good look at Maurice and ask yourself if he's truly the man you want to spend the rest of your life with."

Their mother pushed open the door. From the look on her face, Brandi knew she'd been eavesdropping.

"Of course she wants to be with him," she said. "I can't believe you showed up here at the last minute putting this nonsense in your sister's head just hours before she walks down the aisle."

Their mother put her hand on Erin's shoulders and turned them until her younger daughter was facing the vanity's mirror. "You're the most beautiful bride I've ever seen," she said. "And this wedding is going to be the happiest event of your life."

Adam paid the taxi driver, adding a generous tip to the fare.

"Are you sure I can't help you take your bags inside?"

"No, thanks."

The Ellison Estate employed a household staff to take care of it, Adam thought, looking up at the mansion he'd called home up until a few weeks ago.

He'd decided it would be more convenient to have the driver bring him to the family estate rather than his condo. He could pick up one of his other cars as well as a tux to wear to Brandi's sister's wedding.

Before he could fish his keys out of his pocket, the door to the main house swung open.

"Mr. A!" Thomas Gayle, better know as the Ellison household's "chief of staff," greeted him with a wide smile and a slap on the back. With a house occupied with all men named Ellison, the staff had adopted the habit of calling them by their first initial. Only his late father was the exception. He had always been Mr. Ellison.

"Chief." Adam used the name both the Ellisons as well

as the rest of the household employees called Thomas. He'd worked for them nearly two decades, and while the Ellisons ran a major corporation, Thomas Gayle ran the sprawling estate.

"So how did the baking competition go?"

"Second place," Adam said, but the judge's comment comparing his cake to his late grandfather's still made him feel like the big winner.

"That's great." Thomas looked around, and then lowered his voice. "We've all had our fingers crossed for you. Well, at least the staff did."

"Thanks, man. It's good to see you."

"You, too, sir," he said. "I saw the bags. Does this mean you're back for good? I'll have them sent up to your suite and unpacked immediately."

Adam shook his head. "No, I just came to pick up a few things. The bags are leaving with me."

"Sorry to hear it, sir. We miss you around here. The house isn't the same without you."

"Now that the competition is over, I promise to stop in more often."

Adam took the stairs two at a time up to the suite of rooms he'd occupied on the second story. Here, his closet alone was bigger than the entire condo he lived in now. He went to the rack in the walk-in closet that held the tuxedos he wore primarily to charity fundraising events and pulled one, and then he scrambled around the huge walk-in closet for shoes and matching accessories.

Having gathered everything he needed, Adam was about to walk through a side door to the six-car garage when his uncle called his name.

"Chief said you were here, so I'm sure your brother has already informed you about the mess with your friend,

Zeke Holden, and the Brooks girl," Uncle Jonathan said without preamble.

Adam heaved a sigh before turning to his uncle. He'd assumed the elder Ellison would be at his downtown office today. Just his luck the old goat was home.

"I heard," Adam said, not really in the mood for another showdown with his uncle. Jade and Zeke were married now. The Brooks Brand deal was off the table. It was time for his uncle to move on.

"So I guess you came to rub my nose in it."

"Actually, I just came to pick up some of my things." Adam held up the cloth suit bag containing his tux. "So, your nose is safe from me."

"Humph, I thought you'd be itching to take a bite out of my hide after the way we've been butting heads the last few months. If I were in you shoes, I'm not sure I could be so magnanimous." His uncle shoved his hands in his pants pockets and looked down at the polished, marble floor.

"Look, Uncle Jonathan, I'm sorry the deal fell through and the Holdens got Brooks Brand, but there'll be other deals. Ones I don't have to sell myself into marriage to seal."

His uncle looked up, eyes wide. "Hold on a second. Exactly when did you speak with your brother?"

"I've been in Paris since Friday, but Kyle came by my place before I left."

"So you don't know?"

"Know what?"

"Let's go into my office, son," Uncle Jonathan said. "We need to talk."

Son. What in the hell was going on? Adam put the suit bag down and followed his uncle to the wing of the house they used to conduct business from home.

Adam glanced at his watch as he sat in the armchair

facing his uncle's massive oak desk. He'd been in the room hundreds of times to discuss business with his uncle and always noted the lack of personal effects. Not one plant, photograph or even a personalized coffee mug.

So the new addition caught his eye, a framed black-and-white photograph on the desk. He reached over and picked it up. He'd never seen it before. It was of two young boys dressed in short pants and striped button-down shirts. Both had massive ice cream cones in their hands and huge smiles on their faces.

The large leather chair behind his uncle's desk squeaked as he eased his bulk into it. He looked at the photo Adam held.

"The one on the left with the gap-toothed smile is your father. He'd lost two baby teeth that day and was terrified they wouldn't grow back, so your grandmother scraped together enough change to take us out for ice cream."

Adam stared at the photo a moment before putting it back on the desk. It was hard for him to reconcile the smiling child with the CEO father he'd grown up around.

"So what's going on?" he asked.

"Your pigheadedness saved our ass, that's what," his uncle said. "Brooks Brand is broke."

Adam straightened and leaned forward in his chair. "But they can't be. Our accountants reviewed their books just months ago."

"Cooked books, with some very creative accounting," Uncle Jonathan said.

"Brooks had to have known we would have eventually found out."

"But by then you would have been his son-in-law, and he was banking on us not pursuing legal or criminal action on your new in-laws," his uncle said. "That's why he was so eager to make his pretty daughter a part of the deal.

All that jazz about the merging of two fortunes in family dynasty was bull."

Adam couldn't believe his ears.

"They say old man Holden nearly had a stroke when he found out the only millions his new daughter-in-law comes with are bills and her family's company is on the brink of bankruptcy."

Adam's thoughts immediately turned to Zeke. He must be beside himself. Part of him wanted to reach out to his old friend, but it wasn't his place. Zeke had a wife to turn to for comfort now.

"That's a lot to take in. I'm still stunned."

His uncle crossed his arms over his stomach. "I'm just glad you refused to let me or anyone else pressure you. If you'd given in, we'd be the ones with this nightmare on our hands." Then his uncle leaned forward in his seat. "I can't be certain if your father is staring down or up at us, but I do know he's very proud of you right now."

"Thanks for saying that, Uncle Jonathan. It means a lot to me."

"Enough for you to return to Ellison Industries?"

Adam shook his head. "I'm going through with my plans to open a patisserie."

His uncle nodded, surprisingly accepting of his decision. "The lawyers will be in touch about your inheritance. It's time you had what's rightfully yours."

The two men stood and Adam shook his uncle's out-stretched hand.

"Maybe you could come home now or at least come by for dinner," his uncle said. "I know your brother and the staff miss you."

Adam nodded. "Dinner would be good. I have someone special I'd like you all to meet."

Chapter 19

Between the Paris weekender and worrying her sister was making a big mistake, thoughts of Wesley hadn't entered Brandi's mind.

Until now.

She looked past candelabras alight with white candles and standing vases of red roses decorating the church vestibule to see her ex-fiancé staring right at her. He was decked out in a black tux and standing in the very same building he'd shunned on their would-have-been wedding day.

It was showdown time.

Brandi had imagined the moment at least a hundred times over the months, and she waited a beat for an onslaught of emotions to hit her at seeing him again.

And waited.

However, the fiery anger she used to push past the burning in her lungs as she jogged all those cold winter days didn't ignite. Nor did the vengefulness she'd summoned to propel herself through endless calisthenics surge through her body.

Instead, she couldn't stop the fit of laughter bubbling up in her throat.

She'd put herself through all kinds of hell over *him*.

Brandi took a good hard look at the man who had loomed large in her mind since he'd dumped her. Not only was he shorter than she remembered, it seemed the pounds she'd busted her butt losing had taken up residency on a new spot—his burgeoning gut.

"Hello, Brandi."

His eyes flitted about the room nervously. They hadn't seen each other since the day before their own wedding, and her missing last night's rehearsal dinner had left no opportunity for them to break the ice before having to walk down the church aisle together.

"Wes." She dabbed at the corner of her eye with a finger to keep the tears of laughter forming in her eyes at bay.

"What's so funny?" he asked.

But a more important question entered Brandi's mind. *Why did she ever allow herself to settle for Wesley?* The inner voice she'd allowed to be shushed far too long roared in her ears.

The same voice had whispered *you can do better* only to be drowned out by the kudos she'd received for being lucky enough to land a college-educated, professional black man with a good job and no children.

"Hang on to him, girl." The well-meaning words and a barrage of similar ones had rained on her like confetti in a victory parade.

Even her mother had thrown some rare praise her way. "You're lucky. He works for a well-known business magazine," she'd said. "The best one of my friend's daughters could do after she cracked thirty was a divorced factory worker with three kids."

"Brandi, did you hear me? I asked you what was so funny?" Wesley repeated.

"Nothing." She shook her head. "Just a private joke."

Then finally, the overwhelming wave of emotion she'd braced herself for since she saw her ex washed over her. Only it wasn't any of the ones she'd expected.

All Brandi felt was a tremendous sense of relief.

Relief he hadn't shown up on their wedding day.

Relief she wasn't his wife.

And relief she'd finally had someone who loved her "as is." Not once had she had felt like she had to bend, shape or mold herself to try to catch, please or hold on to Adam.

"You look good." Her ex's eyes skimmed over the once breathing-room-only maid-of-honor dress, which now fit easily. "Really good."

She thanked him for the compliment, which didn't seem to matter as much as she'd envisioned it would.

"So, how's married life?" Brandi asked and then couldn't resist. "Did you bring Tasty along with you today?"

"Um, it's Candy," Wesley corrected. "We didn't want to make things any more awkward, so we decided it would be best if she stayed in Atlanta."

Her mother came over. Jolene frowned at Wesley before telling them the ceremony would be starting soon.

She took Brandi by the arm. "I can't believe you invited that playboy neighbor of yours," she hissed. "I just saw him in the sanctuary."

"Oh, good," Brandi said, relieved to know Adam had made it to the church. She'd been so occupied helping Erin and her mother with the last-minute wedding checklist and then getting dressed herself, she'd only talked to him briefly on the phone since they'd parted at the airport earlier.

Thankfully, her mother was pulling double duty as both wedding coordinator and mother of the bride and was called away before she could comment further.

Wesley looked down at the carpet before looking back at her. "I know this is too little, too late, but I'm sorry for the way I handled everything. I should have told you about Candy sooner. I'd always planned to break it off with her before the wedding, but when I went to do it, I realized I wanted the bad girl more than I loved the good one."

Brandi bit back annoyance and found herself in the position of nearly feeling sorry for Tasty...Candy or whatever her name, because she'd been the unlucky girlfriend to land this booby prize.

"Don't try to rewrite history, Wes. You didn't have the guts to tell me face-to-face. Your poor mother told me and apologized for you."

"But I'm apologizing myself now."

Brandi was saved from telling him exactly what he could do with his sad excuse of an apology by the return of her own mother telling them it was time to start.

Minutes later, the players were all in place at the altar in front of an audience of three hundred well-wishers. Spotting Adam in the church pews looking especially handsome in his tux made the walk up the aisle on Wesley's arm bearable for Brandi.

She glanced at her sister. To say Erin was a beautiful bride would have been an understatement. Her hair and makeup were perfect, and the sequins in her fitted dress shimmered in the candlelight.

"Dearly beloved, we are gathered here today..." The reverend started the preamble leading up to the vows.

Brandi continued to look at her sister. Had Erin thought

about anything she'd said to her earlier? When her sister looked at Maurice was she truly thinking about spending the rest of her life with him?

Brandi's gut said no, and the temptation was strong, very strong, to grab her baby sister by the arm and drag her up the rose-petal-strewn aisle they'd just marched down.

But Erin was a grown woman, and she'd made her choice. All Brandi could do was live with it.

The reverend's voice droned as he addressed Maurice "…For better or worse, for richer or poorer, in sickness and in health. And forsaking all others, be faithful only to her so long as you both shall live?"

"I do," Maurice confirmed.

He wasn't a bad guy, Brandi thought, as he smiled down at her sister. Maybe over time he'd grow less domineering. Besides, if Erin could roll with the way he bossed her around, she'd have to roll with it, too, especially now that he was moments away from being family.

"And do you, Erin Marie Collins…" the reverend began and ended with the question, "so long as you both shall live?"

The corner of Erin's mouth holding up her smile twitched, but otherwise she remained motionless and silent as seconds ticked into minutes.

"Erin," Maurice whispered, nudging her with his elbow.

"I…I don't think I can do this," Erin whispered.

"Don't be ridiculous," Maurice hissed through a clenched-toothed smile. "You're just nervous. Just say 'I do' and we'll go enjoy our reception."

Brandi held her breath until she saw her sister's face take on the contrite look it always did right before she agreed to do whatever Maurice wanted.

"Well, Erin, what do you say?" The reverend gave an uncomfortable chuckle.

"No."

The softly spoken word echoed off the church's high ceilings, setting off a collective gasp inside the sanctuary, and all eyes were on Erin as she ran back up the aisle.

"Not again," Brandi heard her mother cry out.

She wasn't sure how Adam managed to get through the throng of people abandoning the church pews, to either check on Jolene or get to the vestibule and fire up their cell phones to spread the latest Collins gossip, but Brandi was grateful to find Adam at her side.

"You okay?"

Stunned, Brandi could only nod, but as her brain caught up to her eyes she smiled. "Yes, I'm fine," she said. "And I believe my sister is, too."

"What can I do to help you right now?"

Brandi touched a hand to his chest. "Thanks, but there's nothing for you to do here," she said. "I need to make sure my mom and sister are okay, and then I'll meet you at home."

"Are you sure?"

Brandi nodded, and he kissed her before disappearing into the crowd. She stood there for a moment trying to decide whom to go to first. Her mother seemed to be surrounded, so she opted to look for Erin.

"Brandi." A hand on her arm stopped her, and she shrugged it off.

"What do you want, Wesley?" she asked. "I need to find my sister."

"That guy, kissing you." There was a hint of surprise in his voice she guessed wasn't from Erin's hurried exit. "How in the world do *you* know *him?*"

Brandi rolled her eyes skyward. Did her ex think he was the only one who could move on?

"Is *that* who you were with in Paris and couldn't make it to the rehearsal dinner?" Wesley pressed.

Remembering she was in church, Brandi bit back a snarky retort. "Yes, I went to Paris with him," she said. "What's it to you?"

"My reporter's been trying to get an interview with that guy for over two years."

"What?"

"As you undoubtedly know, your boyfriend's family owns one of the region's largest corporations. He's worth millions."

She burst out laughing. "Wesley, you've obviously got him mixed up with someone else. He's not whoever you seem to think he is," Brandi said. "The man you just saw is…"

"Adam Ellison," Wesley finished. "As in Ellison Industries."

Adam hadn't wanted to leave Brandi, but gave her the space she needed to focus on her family.

He grabbed the television remote and flipped through the sports channels. He settled on a basketball game, although it was little more than white noise.

Tonight he planned to finally fill Brandi in on his background. He'd briefly considered putting it off, especially after today's events, but the longer he waited the harder it would be for her to understand why he hadn't been up front with her sooner.

Adam heard a light knock on the door and switched off the remote. He took one look at Brandi, who underneath her coat was still dressed in her wedding finery, and wished he had stayed at her side.

Her eyes were red-rimmed as if she'd been crying.

The aftermath of her sister's flight from the altar must

have been more grueling than she'd anticipated, Adam thought, pulling her into his arms.

The soft body that usually melted into his embrace stiffened. He dropped a kiss on the top of her head. It had been a very long day for her.

"How's your sister?"

"Erin's fine. She's spending the night with her girlfriends." Brandi followed him to the dining room, but didn't make a move to unbutton her coat or sit down.

"And your mother?"

"Last time I saw her she was leading a conga line at what was supposed to be Erin's reception."

"So things turned out okay, right?"

"For them," she said matter-of-factly. "I've answered your questions, now how about you answer mine?"

"Yeah, sure," Adam said, puzzled by her odd behavior.

Brandi reached into her bag, pulled out a sheath of papers and shoved them into his hands. Damn, he thought, flipping through the results of a Google search.

His gaze returned to her face and what he saw in them was worse than anger or hurt. *Disillusion.*

"Who are you?" Her eyes and tone held none of the warmth he'd grown accustomed to.

"The same person I was before you decided to do an internet search on me."

Brandi shook her head. "The thing is I actually believed you were an honest, direct, what-you-see-is-what-you-get kind of guy. It never occurred to me to search you," she said, "until my ex informed me the man I knew as an unemployed, aspiring pastry chef was actually a multimillionaire with a stake in the region's largest corporation."

"Most women wouldn't consider it a negative," Adam replied. "In fact, most women would be thrilled to learn the man who loved her had millions at his disposal, and she could have her heart's desire."

"Up until a few hours ago, I thought I'd already had my heart's desire—a man who was impeccable with his word. One I could trust enough to open that same heart to, because he never lied to me. Turns out you're like all the rest, and I simply hadn't caught you in a lie yet."

"I never once lied to you, Brandi. I have been living off my savings, money I worked hard for despite my family connection to the corporation. I was indeed an executive for a household-goods company, and I left to pursue my long-held dream."

She shook her head. "In my book, sidestepping the truth is still a lie. A lie of omission is still a lie."

Adam wouldn't fight her on it. In her position, he'd feel the exact same way about someone averting the truth. Like Zeke had done with him.

"And to think, all this time I'd actually admired you for having the guts to walk away from your job. But you didn't quit a soulless day job to stop humping for the man. *You are the man.*"

Up until now, Adam had only felt deep regret over hurting her, but her last words really got under his skin.

"The man?" he asked her incredulously. Brandi didn't know the half of it. "My late father was what you would refer to as *the man,* and as his firstborn son I was expected to work ten times harder and twenty times longer than anyone else in his empire."

She poked a finger against his chest. "But I shared it all with you. I told you about my father and my grandmother, getting dumped at the altar, my business. And it turns out you shared nothing with me."

He caught her hand and held it against his chest. "True, I didn't share my background or financial status with you, but I did share everything that was truly important to me. I've dated many women, but you're the first I've ever introduced to my grandmother."

"So why didn't you tell me?" Brandi whispered.

"Would you have banged on my door at three in the morning to tell me off if you had known I was one of *the Ellisons?* Would you have shared all those things with me if you had known my financial status?"

She dropped her chin to her chest before looking up at him again. "I'm no gold digger."

"I know you're not, sweetheart, but can you honestly say you would have treated me the same if you had known? Or would you have written me off as someone from a different world who would never fit into yours?"

"I don't know." Brandi drew her hand back. "You never gave me that chance."

"You're not the only one who carries baggage from the past. You had a bad breakup. I've had a lifetime of people with their own agenda trying to get close to me," he said. "You were so refreshing, so different. I fell for you from the first moment I saw you. And I wanted you to see me, just me, and decide if you wanted me, too."

"But in Paris, after I told you I loved you. Why didn't you trust me enough to tell me then?"

"I didn't want to ruin the moment. I was going to tell you tonight. You believe me, don't you?"

Brandi reached into her other coat pocket, placed his SUV key on the dining room table.

"I don't know what to believe anymore." She turned away from him and walked out of the door.

Chapter 20

Thanks to the sheer exhaustion brought on by jet lag and drama, Brandi slept well into the afternoon the next day.

But as the deep, dreamless sleep ended, reality came crashing back. She and Adam were through, and it made her heart physically ache.

There would be no solace in chocolate this time. It was now synonymous with a man that up until yesterday she believed she had a future with.

Brandi reached for her workout gear. A run followed by a torture session with Heather would leave her too exhausted to think about him or anything else.

The shrill ring of her home phone shattered the silence. Brandi heaved a sigh, and picked up the cordless in her bedroom. She could only put off the real world for so long.

"I'm trying to reach Brandi Collins," the crisp voice on the line said.

"This is she."

"Please hold for Ms. Todd."

Brandi dropped the sneakers she was holding in her other hand. Yesterday, she'd been so consumed with Erin's wedding and discovering Adam's true background, she had completely forgotten to return Lina Todd's call.

Seconds later, the woman whose career and designs she'd long admired came onto the line and briefly introduced herself. Like Lina Todd needed any introduction, Brandi thought.

"The staff at my foundation reviewed over a hundred applications and videos, but yours was the one they brought to my attention. Like them, I'm impressed with what you've done with Arm Candy, and I think it's time we got it out of your spare room," she said.

Still trying to absorb the fact she was actually having a conversation with Lina Todd, it was all Brandi could do to squeeze a thank you beyond the lump in her throat.

"As you know, my foundation is dedicated to giving talented women fashion entrepreneurs the financial leg up they need to succeed when banks aren't an option," the designer said. "We're offering you a thirty-five-thousand-dollar microloan, and I'll be checking in with you once a month for the first year. Maybe I can help you avoid some of the potholes I stumbled into when I was first getting started."

"Thank you, Ms. Todd. I can't tell you how much this means to me," Brandi said.

"You're very welcome," she said. "You must be excited to finally be able to lease the retail space I saw in the video."

"Actually, it's no longer available," Brandi said. "I'll be scouting out a new location."

She hoped it wouldn't make the woman change her mind about her offer.

"I've been on your website, Miss Collins. Your designs are fresh and fun and allowing customers to select their own colors and fabric is a fabulous twist. I think it's a twist women will go out of their way to take advantage of and you'll succeed in any location."

A few minutes later, Lina was gone and Brandi was talking to her assistant, who said Brandi would receive the loan paperwork the next morning.

Brandi did an impromptu happy dance. She could hardly wait to go next door and tell… Then she remembered. She couldn't go to Adam. Not after last night.

But he had gone out of his way to help.

She shook off the thought. He'd lied to her. Case closed.

Picking up her running shoes, she quickly put them on. What she needed to do now was clear her head. She grabbed her keys and pulled open the door, only to see her mother on the other side of it poised to knock.

"Good," Jolene Collins said. "You're here."

"Where else would I be?"

"I thought you might be next door with that new man of yours." Her mother walked in, her eyes flitting around the living and dining rooms like she was looking for something. "So is he here?"

"Who?" Brandi asked. She'd thought her mother would still be lamenting, having pulled together two weddings and having no married daughters to show for it.

"You know who."

"Oh, the unemployed, loser gigolo who's only seeing me for my money?" Brandi asked.

"Don't be silly. He doesn't need to work." Her mother smiled sweetly. "You could have told me he was one of *those* Ellisons. Anyway, I thought it was time for us to be properly introduced, seeing that you two are so close."

"That's not necessary," Brandi began.

"Of course it is," Jolene cut her off. Her mother clasped her hands together as if in prayer. "An Ellison, I can hardly believe it. That's way more prestigious than a doctor. You should have seen my friends' faces when Wesley let the cat out of the bag. It was priceless."

Brandi stared at her mother in disbelief. Jolene pulled a magazine from her purse and turned to a page of an aerial photo of two mansions flanked by trees and surrounded by acres of greenery.

"This is his *real* home, Brandi," she said. "Can you imagine living in a place like this with a staff waiting on you?"

Brandi felt the first stumble off the high horse of self-righteousness she'd ridden on out of Adam's condo last night. Is this the kind of behavior his millions bought him? Even from people Brandi would have thought would know better, like her own mother.

"Mom," Brandi started, but Jolene talked over her.

"First we need to get some more of those pounds off that behind of yours, perhaps a new chic haircut, more makeup and some sexier clothes. I'll show you how to give that other woman sniffing around him some competition."

Brandi's high horse stumbled again. Adam had loved her "as is" and had never required her to be anyone but herself. Even in scruffy sweats, he'd still wanted her.

"We broke up," she said, wishing she hadn't been so sanctimonious with him last night.

Jolene's eyes widened in horror as Brandi finally got through to her.

"He's back with that woman I saw him kissing, isn't he? I should have known."

Brandi heaved a weary sigh and walked toward her door.

"Where are you going?" her mother asked. "We need

to talk. We need to put our heads together and come up with a plan for you to get that millionaire… I mean that man back."

Brandi spun around. "Mom, after our talk a few weeks back I made peace with the fact that you are who you are, instead of who I want you to be," she said. "Now you're going to have to do the same with me."

"But…" her mother began.

"My relationship or nonrelationship with Adam is none of your business," she said firmly. "You've already raised me. I'm a grown-up. I don't need you to do it again."

"Brandi!" Jolene huffed.

"Are we clear, Mom? Good," she said, not waiting for her mother to close her shocked mouth to answer. "Now I'm going for a run. You can let yourself out."

A mile into her trek Brandi veered from the running path she usually took with Heather in the park and instead ran through her neighborhood toward the community's town center.

She remembered how busy the area had been the night she and Adam came out to Jolt's for coffee. The retail space here was in brand-new buildings, the area was up-and-coming, and in walking distance of her condo.

In short, the perfect place for Arm Candy Handbags had been right under her nose all along.

Slowing her pace to a walk, she approached one of the available storefronts in a brown brick building on the same block as Jolt's. She imagined a storefront window display of her handbags.

Pulling her cell phone from her jacket pocket, she dialed the leasing agent's phone number and left a message. She didn't want to miss out on this space.

At least her business life was finally looking up, even if her love life had returned to nonexistent. She opted to walk instead of run the short distance back to her condo. All the day's good news for Arm Candy rang hollow without Adam to share it with. He'd helped her so much. But after the way she'd berated him last night, he probably didn't want anything to do with her.

Brandi had been so deep in thought she hadn't seen Adam standing on the landing of their building until it was too late. All she could do was simply stare at him. Lines etched his eyes, and he looked tired. She resisted the urge to smooth a hand over the after-five shadow clinging to his jaw.

"I stopped by your place looking for you. Your mother was leaving and told me you were out running, so I came out to find you."

He reached for her hand. "I'm sorry I misled you, Brandi. If you give me another chance, I promise my life will be an open book to you," he said. "Do you think you can ever forgive me?"

She nodded. "Only if you can forgive me for being so pious and self-righteous last night. I don't care what Google says about you or your bank balance. Unemployed or millionaire, I love you, Adam Ellison."

Adam pulled her into his arms and captured her mouth in a kiss that left her insides as soft and gooey as his award-winning lava cake.

"If you still want that Green Hills location for Arm Candy, I'll buy you the entire block," he said.

Brandi shook her head. "That's not necessary."

"Consider it a wedding present."

"Wedding present?" Brandi asked, unsure of what he meant.

"That is, if you'll marry me."

"Yes!" Brandi threw her arms around his neck and planted a kiss on his lips.

"Is that yes to my proposal or my buying you a building?" Adam asked when they came up for air.

Brandi laughed. "I happily accept your proposal, but will have to decline your offer of the building," she said, her arms still looped around his neck.

"What good is having money if I can't spoil my wife-to-be?"

Brandi shook her head. "It's not that. The Lina Todd microloan came through. I can rent a location myself," she said. "In fact, I'm looking at a storefront right here in the community's town center."

"Congratulations on the microloan. I can't think of a business more deserving than yours," he said.

"I couldn't have done it without you." She inhaled the faint scent of chocolate as she snuggled into his embrace. "As a matter of fact, I was thinking the town center would be the perfect place for a patisserie."

"Really now?" Adam raised a brow, then kissed her again. "How about we look into it when we all get back from Hawaii?"

"Hawaii? Who's going to Hawaii?"

"Me, you, your mother and sister and my brother and uncle."

"Huh? I don't get it."

"Sorry, sweetheart, but I'm not taking a chance on another Collins woman non-wedding."

Adam pulled his cell phone from his pocket. "I'm calling our pilot. I want us all aboard the Ellison jet this afternoon, and the two of us in front of a minister as soon as we can make it legal," he said. "So what do you have to say to that, Brandi Collins?"

"I do."

* * * * *

*Have yourself a sexy little holiday
with three favorite authors in...*

Merry SEXY CHRISTMAS

BEVERLY JENKINS
KAYLA PERRIN
MAUREEN SMITH

**May your days—and nights—be merry and bright
with these brand-new stories, written by three of the
genre's hottest authors, perfect for adding a dash of
sizzle to the Christmas season!**

Available November 2012 wherever books are sold!

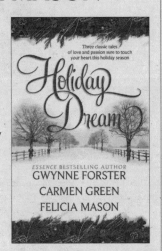

REQUEST YOUR FREE BOOKS!

2 FREE NOVELS PLUS 2 FREE GIFTS!

KIMANI™ ROMANCE

Love's ultimate destination!

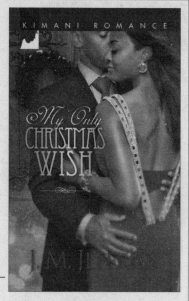